DANCING
around the
HILL

DANCING
around the
HILL

PART 1 The Gregorian Affair
PART 2 The Syndicate

'Like moths flitting around a candle flame on a late summer's eve,
they pirouette, bow and dance around the power on the hill'

EDWARD MASTRONARDI

DANCING AROUND THE HILL
PART 1 THE GREGORIAN AFFAIR PART 2 THE SYNDICATE

iUniverse books may be ordered through booksellers or by contacting:

iUniverse
1663 Liberty Drive
Bloomington, IN 47403
www.iuniverse.com
1-800-Authors (1-800-288-4677)

ISBN: 978-1-4917-7778-7 (sc)
ISBN: 978-1-4917-7913-2 (e)

Library of Congress Control Number: 2015916932

Print information available on the last page.

iUniverse rev. date: 10/14/2015

CONTENTS

PART 2
The Syndicate 161

PART 1
The Gregorian
Affair

PROLOGUE

Anthony Muldoon sat alone in the National Press Club lounge, finishing the last of his ritual Friday evening double scotches. He hunched bear-like in a large armchair and enjoyed the warm glow created by the scotch. He was also pleased by the multiple compliments he had received throughout the evening from his out-of- town newspaper reporter colleagues over his newspaper series, particularly the explosive articles on the Gregorian affair scandal, which had hit the Ottawa scene like a bomb shell. His articles had helped implicate the minority liberal government, leading to its politically crushing defeat in the recent election. Small groups of men huddled around the randomly spaced tables, talking in low voices, oblivious to the squishy hum of the early November traffic splashing its way along Wellington street in the teeming rain.

Standing up, stretching his arms over his head with a jaw cracking yawn, turned around facing the large partially draped window behind his worn leather chair. He stared at the spotlight-bathed gothic towers of the Parliament buildings perched on the high bluffs overlooking the Ottawa river, his large Irish face creased with a smug look. Yes, his scoop on the Gregorian immigration scandal was a god-send for him; a syndicated column in the Ottawa Tribune, a generous bonus, a raise, the envy of his peers. It also permitted he and his grateful wife moving from their shabby center town apartment to a luxurious one in one of Ottawa's better addresses, also housing two cabinet ministers and several lawyers in between wives. Slouched back in his chair, bent over picking up his half-emptied glass of scotch from the low table in front. He proposed another toast to the unknown source of his good fortune. Grunting at the small roll of fat bordering his belt, promised himself laying off the club's calorie filled Friday night menu.

Looking at his watch, it was nearly ten, his wife, Anne would soon be driving into the underground garage of their apartment overlooking the Rideau canal, Friday evening her shopping and chatting meetings with girlfriends permitting his weekly 'Thank God it's Friday' sessions at the club. Gulping down the rest of his drink rose to leave when the club's speaker system rudely shattered the quiet, "Mister Muldoon, telephone for Tony Muldoon."

Making his way picking up the phone at the end of the bar, a few curious faces staring at him as he passed by, their recognition giving him a feeling of warm satisfaction, a new experience in his twenty years of working life. Picking up the extension waiting for the bartender's to click before speaking,

"Hello? Muldoon speaking."

"Hello Tony, it's Don Simms. Thought I'd catch you there."

"Well, you're lucky Don, I was just leaving." he replied, hiding his annoyance.

Simms, a ministerial executive assistant, who like others of his kind, frequently contacted him, hoping for a favorable comment about their Minister in his column, one of those 'reliable sources' essential to the media. He enjoyed reflecting the power of greater men, learning to use this perverse form of influence to full advantage, becoming a master of the ' I'll scratch your back if you'll scratch mine school'; in his case, if he gave you something be sure giving him something back.

"Tony, you'll never guess who the Prime Minister is appointing Secretary to the Cabinet and Clerk of the Privy Council," Simms demanded eagerly.

Hiding his irritation Tony mentioned a few speculated in a recent column.

"No, you're dead wrong!" lowering his voice, Simms replied, "It's an old buddy of yours!"

Muldoon's scotch induced feeling of well-being died, replaced by a gnawing dread, "You can't mean Scott Beaumont?"

"As sure as hell! How does that grab you?" he chortled, knowing there was no love lost between Muldoon and Beaumont which sometimes found itself in Tony's Dancing around the Hill column in the Tribune.

"Well, it's quite a surprise, thanks for telling me Don, I owe you one."

Hanging up the phone, Muldoon, shook his head, looking stunned gasped in disbelief. He was aware of the poorly kept secret that the man being replaced, on the job after only three months, was seriously ill. Scott Beaumont's appointment to the top public service job in the country was Incredible! Not that he any doubts about suave, charming Beaumont doing well under the new regime. A junior Deputy Minister appointed to be the Prime Minister's right hand man? Unbelievable! Beaumont would not only be responsible for providing the Prime Minster advice and support on his prerogatives and responsibilities for the organization of the Government of Canada, he would be managing the activities of the Cabinet, including its numerous committees. Appointing Beaumont was a far cry from that of public administration giants wielding such power in the past.

Muldoon, his deep seated angry resentment welling up, sweating profusely despite the coolness in the lounge, leaned against the bar, thinking bitterly, "Why David Preston, the former government's Cabinet Secretary, was a Rhodes scholar, had a law degree, and Harvard MBA. His superb articles on public administration were published by several prestigious international journals. Married to one of the most charming intelligent woman in Ottawa, the Preston's were close friends of the former Liberal Prime Minister, Donald Porter." Muldoon, his hands trembling, had trouble signing his bar chit.

Stepping into the cloakroom adjoining the bar, stumbled over a carpet reached for his raincoat, putting it on over his stocky frame, "The probably think I'm Loaded." he mused ruefully, pulling his Donegal hat over a mass of unruly red hair, reluctantly making his way out the main entrance into the rain-swept night. Muldoon, walking briskly along Wellington towards Elgin street, jogged across its wide expanse towards the National Arts Centre, dodging through the flickering headlight beams of the slow moving traffic, the chill of the night penetrating his trench coat.

Momentarily pausing to catch his breath, stared thoughtfully at the silent cluster of illuminated military statues forming the centre piece of the Cenotaph, breathing deeply, headed for the entrance of the pathway bordering the west side of the Rideau canal. The streets, now nearly empty, most of the civil servants, who thickly populated the centre of the city during the day, had long since returned to the snug comfort of their suburban homes, leaving a few downtown dwellers scurrying along the glistening wet streets like drenched mice seeking shelter. Approaching the telephone booths, standing like sentinels outside the pathway entrance, realized he'd better call his paper adding the Beaumont item to his Monday column. Fumbling in his pocket for change, telephoned the night editor, Roger Lemieux.

When Muldoon finished Lemieux asked, "Is that all, Tony? Just a mention with no comment?"

"Yes, just a mention. That's all!" Muldoon snapped!

"Okay, okay... you don't have to bite my head off! I'll add it just the way you gave it to me, anything else?" he snapped back.

"Sorry Roger, it's been a bad day."

After hanging up the phone, Tony started walking briskly south along the upper path beside the canal. Striding along the black ribbon-like path, trying unsuccessfully wiping the Beaumont incident from his mind, suddenly his apartment building broke through the darkness, most off the apartments alight. Sighing with relief his was dark, Anne was still out, Tony, sick at the prospect of telling her about Beaumont's appointment, afraid of what he might see in her face. Entering found the plush-carpeted lobby, decorated in an Aztec motif, deserted. Approaching the imitation bronze doors of the elevators, "Montezuma would have hated this." Muldoon said ruefully as the elevator silently deposited him on the 12th floor.

The hallway leading to his apartment was dimly lit by a series of bronze candelabras strung out like torches along one wall. Unlocking his door, entered turning on the hall light, automatically kicking off his wet loafers, shoving his feet into a worn pair of oversized slippers in their usual place beside the door. Shaking the rain out of his coat, hung it up in the closet, shuffled into the living room, turning on an end table lamp, illuminating the living room's beige covered walls covered with an assortment of early Spanish and Mexican bric-a-brac, collected during a recent holiday in Mexico. Sauntering into the kitchen, took a beer out of the fridge, returned to the living room gulping out of the bottle, a habit his wife abhorred.

Just settling comfortably into his high wing-backed leather chair, heard a key turning in the door lock, "Hi honey!" he called, smiling as his wife entered, closing the door.

Removing her heavy tweed coat. "What happened Tony, did the club run out of scotch?" she replied cheerfully, entering the living room, shaking the rain out of shoulder-length thick auburn hair. Seeing the half empty beer bottle in her husband's hand, her green eyes flashed, "Oh Tony! How many times have I begged you to use a glass? You look such a boor drinking like that, besides, haven't you had enough to drink?"

As she stretched out on their comfortable chesterfield, rising from his chair, grinning, her husband countered, "Tough day at day at the shop? If you'll stop your nagging, I'll pour you a glass of wine."

Her voice followed him into the kitchen, "I should take up Jane Price's offer to buy into her boutique, using the money Dad left me."

"You're better off leaving it in the bank earning interest, besides, there are too many other dress boutiques in the city as it is." he replied.

"Perhaps you're right, it would be nice though to be a part owner and not just an employee." she answered, yawning, putting a hand delicately to her mouth. Moments later, Tony, returning with her flute of wine and a glass for his beer, found her sound asleep. Placing her glass on the coffee table in front of the chesterfield, slid lazily into his chair, pouring the rest of his beer into his glass.

Anne's face, softened in sleep, displaying a youthfulness making it unbelievable she was forty. The nostrils of her delicately shaped nose moving gently with her even breathing, her right arm hanging limply over the edge of the chesterfield, her left across her body its hand folded in her lap. Her blouse was partially opened at the neck, her right leg bent over her outstretched left moving her plaid skirt high over her shapely thighs. Staring at her, Tony felt the old surge of hot desire he felt constantly during the early years of their courtship and marriage. So intent looking at her legs, he didn't notice she was awake.

Looking down at her are bared thighs, tugged at her skirt in the embarrassed way all women do seeing a man staring at their legs, "Dirty old man!" she murmured looking deeply into her husband's eyes.

Wanting to take her right then, hesitated, there was no hurry with the rest of the night ahead of them, besides it would be much nicer in bed, he could wait.

"Anything exciting happen at the paper today?" she asked stifling a yawn.

Her casual question shattering Tony's amorous mood, forcibly reminded him of Scott Beaumont's appointment. Briefly deciding remaining silent, changed his mind realizing she, on seeing the item in his Monday column, would wonder why he hadn't told her, considering his silence an act of backsliding after all their effort saving their marriage.

"Well, only one item of interest, Scott Beaumont is being appointed the new Secretary to the Cabinet." he replied tonelessly after a long pause, averting looking at her.

Yawning, she replied, "That's quite a promotion isn't it? I didn't think he had that kind of support from the Conservatives."

Although her reply seemed casual enough, Muldoon's deep seated anger bursting inside of him, snarled, "I don't know a damn thing about his friends political or otherwise! Maybe you do after what you two meant to each other, you should be overjoyed hearing your precious Scott grabbing the biggest brass ring in the

Public Service! You should also know about a strong rumor, he's involved in an affair with his Minister, an attractive female dynamic personality from British Columbia which the paper refused to let me report ."

Seeing the look of frightened dismay on his wife's tear stained face realized he had gone too far, only succeeding in mindlessly destroying their hard work restoring their marriage.

Anne white-faced, leaped to her feet, hands clenched by her sides, shrieked, "You miserable bastard! Oh God, how I hate your petty jealousy! You...you promised!" Unable to face her husband any longer, turned, running down the hall to their bedroom, slamming the door.

Tony, hearing her heart-rending sobs, feeling thoroughly ashamed, followed her desperately hoping she would forgive him, pleading with her through the closed door; it was useless.

"Please leave me alone Tony! Go away!" she begged, sobbing.

Ignoring her pleas, Muldoon threw open the door storming into the room, finding his wife sitting up in the bed, clutching a pillow to her breast, frightened, wide-eyed stared at her husband standing rigidly at the foot of their bed, his face blazing with anger, the large vein above his right temple throbbing. Suddenly his anger evaporated into a surging wave of shame an d guilt, not having seen her this unhappy since, soon after their marriage, learned she was unable to have children. Turning quickly, stepped quietly out of the room gently closing the door, saying, "I better leave her alone."

Slowly making his way to the dining room, cursed at his stupidity for having been such a damn fool raising the old specter that nearly destroyed their marriage, a specter he had sworn to bury forever. "No use crying over spilt milk!" he sighed. Grabbing a bottle of scotch and a highball glass out of the liquor cabinet, retraced his steps, moved quietly down the hallway past the bedroom door stepping into his study.

As usual the room was a mess, his mess, books, files, papers and old newspaper clippings strewn everywhere. The only quality piece of furniture in the partially paneled, bookcase-lined room was his father's large oak desk. Wearily collapsing into the sole chair in the study, a well-worn leather recliner, pouring himself a stiff scotch, looked around the room, its ceiling high bookcases filled with a variety of publications gathered over the years. Hung on the only remaining wall space was his fading Arts degree. Sagging dejectedly in his chair, knew his wife was crying herself to sleep. He fully understood what was really troubling him, it wasn't Anne. Draining his glass, tilting back his chair, staring sightlessly at the ceiling, cursed the day Scott Beaumont had entered their lives.

CHAPTER 1

Scott Beaumont

Scott Beaumont absorbed reading the latest draft of his paper outlining a regional development strategy for the federal government was oblivious to the pall of sticky July heat permeating his dingy office. The rays of blinding light streaming through the battered venetian blind covering the half-opened window beside his desk outlined his finely chiseled features, his long aquiline nose, bespeaking his Norman-English ancestry, the blue of his widely spaced eyes, accentuated by a head of thick, carefully brushed black hair. Looking concerned, wondering if the Assistant Deputy Minister he reported to, James Ferguson, had spotted the typo error in the copy sent to him the previous day. When they met later that afternoon in Ferguson's ornate corner office located in a new government office building, located a few blocks south of Wellington street, learned he had.

"Look here Beaumont, I don't know what to make of this sloppy work, look at this!" he growled, shaking the last page of the report in Beaumont's face, "I'm surprised you didn't pick this typo error before sending this thing to me!"

Struggling to keep his composure, Beaumont quietly replied, "Yes sir, I agree, I should have spotted it, but what about the concept I've put forward, do you agree with it?"

"No I don't, Beaumont! We're not ready for increasing the level of decision-making for our regional directors you propose, besides I seriously doubt the Deputy Minister will agree to it!" throwing it on his desk.

"Just a moment, Mister Ferguson, that's precisely what the Deputy proposed in his briefing last month!" Beaumont protested heatedly.

His puckish face compressed into a worried frown, Ferguson replied, "Well, you'll have to clean it up before I'll pass it on." Continuing in a more accommodating tone, "By the way, what are you doing about the publicity brochures for the program? The Deputy is keen we do a good job on them, the Minister expects it."

"I understand Mister Arnott arranged with the National Defense Deputy for the transfer of one of his information specialists over to us. He's an ex military type, I believe his name is Anthony Muldoon, he's reported to be very good." Beaumont replied.

"How did you find all this out?" Ferguson demanded angrily.

"At a cocktail party last week. He asked me how I was coming along on the project, that's when he told me." Scott replied, raising his eyebrows.

"I suppose Mister Arnott already knows what you're recommending?"

"Yes sir, he does!"

Shrugging his shoulders Ferguson turned his attention to the publicity question, "Muldoon, sounds Irish. I hope he isn't one of those Paddy's likely to make trouble. You know the type I mean!"

Ferguson commented, wrinkling his nose as if there was a bad smell in his office.

Beaumont didn't reply, instead asked, "Is that all Mister Ferguson?"

"Yes, yes, you can go now. Let me see a new draft as soon as possible, along with an outline for the promotional material."

After leaving the building, striding up the street towards his office, Beaumont muttered, "What a strange little man!"

The following morning, as Scott stood looking out his window at the early morning traffic streaming along Wellington street, heard a familiar knock, "Yes Marilyn, please come in." he responded.

In walked his secretary, Marilyn Arnold, a tall leggy brunette, more striking than beautiful, wearing a figure massaging red silk dress, her prominent breasts outlined in bold relief by its tight bodice. "Mister Muldoon has arrived for his eight thirty appointment." she said breathlessly, staring hungrily at Scott.

"Fine Marilyn, show him in, please." he replied with a smile that always made her tingle.

Motioning Muldoon to enter, partially blocking the doorway, forced him to brush by her. As she left, he paused, staring at her well-rounded behind. Looking embarrassed, Tony turned facing his director.

Scott, moved from behind his desk, grinning, "I see you've met our Marilyn, I'm Scott Beaumont." extending his right hand, looked quizzically at the ginger-haired, perspiring, thick-set figure, in a rumpled striped summer suit, standing uncomfortably in front of him. He surmised Muldoon was five or six years his senior, making him around forty-five.

As they shook hands, Muldoon, trying to sound casual, replied, "I'm Anthony but everyone calls me Tony."

"Please take a seat, would you like a coffee?" Beaumont offered.

"No thank you, sir," Muldoon responded sitting down heavily, intimidated by the composed person sitting opposite who seemed impervious to the stifling heat in the room.

"Sir? I haven't been called that since leaving the army."

Tony, distressed replied, "I'm afraid old habits are hard to break."

Putting Muldoon at ease, Scott explained, "Look Tony, we don't stand on ceremony around here. I'm Scott, there is an exception, the branch head, James Ferguson, insisting on Mister or Sir". After commenting on the dinginess of the facilities, Beaumont launched into a no-nonsense, hour-long briefing on his project, its progress to date, what remained to be done and Tony's role in the enterprise, all the time looking directly at him. After finishing, reaching into a drawer withdrew Muldoon's resume, "I see you're an Arts grad from Toronto U, trained as a navigator in the Canadian Air Force staff college entrance, a staff officer at Training command headquarters, impressive! How did you become involved in the writing business?"

"I found I had a flair for it while at Training Command Headquarters getting involved in writing training brochures, recruiting advertisements, news releases, even occasionally draft speeches for air rank officers, that sort of thing." he explained, relaxed, smiling for the first time.

About to continue Scott was interrupted by a call from his secretary, "Mister Beaumont, Mister Ferguson wants to see you right away!"

"Did he say what he wanted me for?" he demanded testily.

"No, only that it was important." she replied nervously.

"Look Tony, I have to leave now, the master doesn't like to kept waiting." Sighing, he rose from his chair.

"I'm looking forward to meeting him." Muldoon responded eagerly.

"Don't be surprised if you're disappointed!" Scott retorted angrily, his blue eyes glittering. Regretting his outburst, softened his tone, "He has a lot on his plate making him seem difficult at times. Look, I'll try to set up a meeting for you when I meet him. By the way, Tony, we start early around here, I'm usually in by eight. We'll pick up where we left off in the morning. Meanwhile, I'll have Marilyn show you where your office is and dig up some project background material for you to read."

CHAPTER 2

Tony Muldoon

Tony's sparsely furnished small office, located a few doors away from Beaumont's, "Not much to look at but a start", he mused, seeing a large file on the well-worn oak desk along with an assortment of office materials including a note pad, pens, pencils and a government telephone directory. Hanging his jacket on the back of the swivel chair behind his desk cursing the heat sat down commencing going through the bulky file. It was after six when he finally left the office and walked to his small apartment arriving home, found his wife Anne busy preparing their supper.

Looking up when she heard him enter cheerfully asked, "How did it go, dear?"

"Fine, fine." he replied, sounding tired laying his heavy briefcase on a chair beside the kitchen table. "My boss Scott Beaumont seems nice enough but his boss, the Assistant Deputy Minister, could be a problem, we'll see, time will tell." he replied stifling s yawn. "What's for supper?"

"I'm afraid it's last night's leftovers, tomorrow will be better.

Tony we'll celebrate your new job with a roast chicken, sweet potatoes and a bottle of white wine."

"That sounds great, I have a lot of reading to do for a meeting to-morrow morning, they start early over there."

Muldoon left early the next morning, careful not disturbing his wife who didn't have to start work as a sales clerk in a popular mid town boutique until ten am. Arriving at his office ahead of Beaumont, continued reviewing the project file, making notes as he did so.

Scott, arriving precisely at eight, walked into Tony's office, smiling, "I see you're also an early riser, Tony. I have a few things to clear up, let's meet in my office at nine, I'll order us some coffee."

Arriving at Beaumont's office at the appointed time, Muldoon found him sitting at a small table in the centre of the room. Looking up Beaumont asked, "Well, Tony, have you been able to go through the file?"

"Yes, last night and this morning, writing some notes, questions and comments." He replied.

"Excellent Tony! Let's get on with it."

Opening he file, Muldoon extracted his notes, replying skeptically, "Well, to begin with, trying to tie in government grants to performance measures similar to those used to measure private sector company productivity, as an indicator of a government program's success strikes me as being impracticable if not impossible."

Shaking his head Beaumont responded, "Not so in the opinion of George Arnott, our Deputy Minister. He has quite a background in statistical quantitative analysis as applied to business performance. He believes a similar analytical technique could be applied to government program performance. I have project team working on that concept. Your job, Tony, is to help us sell this concept not only to the public but to the public service as well."

Still skeptical Muldoon replied, "I still think it will be a hard sell but I'll do my best."

The next several hours were spent coming to grips with how this best could be done as well as reviewing Tony's other observations and comments. That evening, enjoying Anne's roast chicken and white wine, enthusiastically briefed her on his session with Scott Beaumont, finished by saying, "He's quite a guy, Anne! Quite a guy!"

Muldoon, immersing himself in Beaumont's project, spending the next two weeks meeting the other project members. Tony working directly under for Scott, resulted in their spending a lot of time together, during which he discovered a lot about his director's background. He learned that Scott came from a military family, as was his father a Royal Military College graduate, had a Masters degree from Harvard in business administration, married, like Tony, childless. While they enjoyed an after luncheon brandy Scott confided, "I decided to give up the military two years ago. It wasn't an easy decision leaving the regiment my father commanded during the war. He was very put out when I told him. I had made up my mind and that was it!"

A month passed, Muldoon had yet to meet James Ferguson, raised the matter with Beaumont during a luncheon, "I guess the ADM isn't in a hurry to meet me, does he think I have BO?"

"No, nothing like that." Scott replied, "He's a very busy guy, hardly having time to see me. I'm sure he'll want to meet with you when you produce the first draft of the program description brochure. It's only fair that I warn you, he can seem difficult at times, even with me!"

"I'm not so sure! He didn't seem overly impressed with the outline you showed him." Muldoon interjected, looking worried,

"Don't lose any sleep over it Tony, everything will be fine when he sees the final product, from what I've seen so far looks good. When do you think it will be ready for him to see?"

"By the end of next week if I don't have any problems getting it typed."

"Good! If you run into any problems with the pool let me know and I'll have Marilyn do it"

"She can type?" Muldoon queried, grinning.

CHAPTER 3

Muldoon Meets Ferguson

James Ferguson stared at his appointment book, annoyed at having agreed meeting Beaumont with his new man that Paddy Muldoon, to discuss the brochure laying half-opened on his desk. Preferring to have spent the afternoon sailing his sloops sighed listlessly flipping over the brochure's pages when his phone rang.

His secretary nervously reporting, "Mister Ferguson, Mister Beaumont just called saying he can't attend the two o'clock meeting to discuss the brochure. He said Mister Muldoon will attend and should be able to any questions you may regarding its content."

Ferguson snapped, "Indeed! Did he say why he can't attend?"

"Yes, sir, he said the Deputy Minister called wanting to see him at the same time. Shall I let Mister Muldoon know it will be alright?"

"No! Yes, go ahead, tell him to come". Switching off the intercom, snarled, "Damn that Beaumont! He has no business seeing the Deputy over my head. Why should I have to deal with an underling while he socializes with Arnott?"

Seething at the thought of Beaumont meeting with the Deputy, worried he had probably told him the advertising brochure was ready, resentful having to meet with a junior officer. Ferguson bitterly resented Scott's personal relationship with George Arnott, a relationship created by the Deputy having served under Scott's father during the war, He was in a foul humor awaiting Muldoon's arrival.

Making certain not to be late for his appointment, Tony, eager to meet the ADM for the first time, arrived at Ferguson's office ten minutes early. He needn't have bothered, left cooling his heels in the large outer office for thirty minutes.

Finishing a lengthy telephone conversation with the Commodore of his yacht club over an up-coming regatta, Ferguson called his secretary to bring Muldoon in. Tony, ushered into Ferguson's spacious, luxuriously furnished, air conditioned office by his secretary found him hunched over his large, mahogany desk It's gleaming surface clear except for the draft brochure. Ferguson, his large oval shaped head covered with strands of sand colored hair carefully combed over a bald spot, seemed to staring at some point on the floor in front of Muldoon. He suddenly straightened up, motioned Tony to a chair in front of his desk, pointing to the brochure, frowning, asked, "So you're the Muldoon Beaumont told me about. I presume this is your work?"

Tony nervously replied, "Yes, sir, it is."

"Well, Muldoon, you'll have to do better than this! I don't like the way it's written. I'm surprised your director passed it on to me." he snapped in a grating Scottish burr, his thin, pale lips twisted in a sneer.

Tony's throat tightened, his mouth dry, his face flushed a deep red, struggling to control his temper, "But Mister Ferguson, Scott

Beaumont liked my approach and made a lot of helpful suggestions which I incorporated into the text!"

"I'm not here to argue with you Muldoon! I don't like it! It's amateurish, any further discussion will be confined to your superior." dismissed him with a wave of his hand. "Close the door after you tell my secretary I want Beaumont to call me immediately after his meeting with the Deputy."

Leaving the building,Tony exploded, "That son of a bitch! Just who in the hell does he think he is?"

Later that afternoon a crestfallen Muldoon was called into Beaumont's office, "I gather you had a rough time with Ferguson?"

"Rough time? That ignorant little bastard didn't even show the courtesy of saying hello before tearing me apart. Is he like this all the time?"

Ignoring Tony's slur against Ferguson, Scott replied, "He's like that with nearly everybody, at times, even with me. He gave me a rough time too. Let's make a few judicious changes to show we're responsive, I'll take it over to him myself. I'm really sorry he was so rough on you, it wouldn't have happened had I been there."

Tony felt better but disturbed over Ferguson's obvious dislike of him."But why?" he asked himself, "He doesn't even know me!"

On leaving Scott's office, Marilyn handed him a small sealed envelope, inside was a note and an invitation, the note read, 'Truly sorry about this afternoon'. The invitation was to a cocktail party Beaumont was having at his home the following Friday evening. On arriving home, deciding not to tell his wife about his disheartening meeting with Ferguson, handed her Beaumont's invitation.

"Oh Tony, this is wonderful! At last I'll meet that paragon of virtue whose made such an impression on you. I'm so happy both of you work so well together."

Feeing a tinge of jealously, he responded, "Well, I wouldn't call him a paragon of virtue; I have to admit he's great to work with."

Kissing him on the cheek, she replied, smiling, "Well, we both can be thankful for that. Tony, dear, I know just the thing to wear, a lovely black number that just arrived at the shop. I'll buy it tomorrow. I want you to look really nice too, wear your charcoal grey suit, you look great in it." Anne was dying to meet the man who had made such a strong impression on her husband, Scott Beaumont who, in her mind represented the ultimate of success, someone with a great future. His behavior, his cool self control, attributes in direct contrast to those of her husband.

CHAPTER 4

The Cocktail Party

Anne met Tony at a university dance in Toronto, she, a student in her graduating year, he, a newly commissioned navigator in the Royal Canadian Air Force, stationed at a nearby base. At first, Anne found him great fun, handsome looking in uniform, widely popular by his singing and piano playing. Falling in love, they married shortly after she graduated, at her family home in North Toronto. In the beginning they were very happy, she readily adjusting to the life of an air force officer's wife. However, a combination of learning she was unable to conceive, loneliness created by her husband's frequent duty absences, slowness in his career advancement, led to her disenchantment.

On the morning of the day of the cocktail party, Anne, taking the day off from work, went to her hairdresser, receiving the full treatment, hair, facial massage, nails. Before leaving looked into full length mirror, smiling smugly exclaimed, "I don't look half bad at all!"

Coming home early that afternoon, Anne's husband was dazzled by his wife's appearance. He knew she had taken the morning off for the full treatment. As she joined him, he turned and said, "You look stunningly beautiful!"

While driving to the Beaumont residence, situated in a fashionable area in west Ottawa, they speculated on what sort of person Scott's wife would prove to be.

She's probably very beautiful." Anne said quietly.

"Maybe so dear, she couldn't possibly be as beautiful as you look tonight." Tony responded reassuringly.

Arriving at the Beaumont's, impressed by their large Georgian style manor, after finding a place among the cars parked outside, walked up to the house's main entrance, Tony ringing the musical bell beside the large mahogany front door. The door was opened by Scott Beaumont.

Standing slightly behind her husband, Anne caught her breath, seeing the tall darkly handsome figure standing in front of them, said to herself, "So this is Scott Beaumont!"

"Welcome to the manor nice people." he said, smiling as he extended his hand. "Tony, so this is your lovely wife, you never told me how beautiful she is!" Ushering them in."Come, I want you to meet my wife, Carole". Beaumont led them to center of the ornate, beautifully furnished living room, its walls adorned with Italian and English art, where a tall, beautifully dressed, striking looking woman whose shoulder length blonde hair, curled in at the ends framed a classic face was talking to an uncomfortable looking couple, the Fergusons.

As Scott approached her with the Muldoon's in tow, she turned towards them, smiling, "This must be the gem you have working with you, Scott, you must be Tony, and?"

"I'm Anne, Tony's wife. It's a pleasure meeting you Missis Beaumont."

"Carole, please." Turning to the other couple, " I'd like you to meet the Fergusons, James and Martha."

Ferguson reluctantly shaking Tony's hand, muttered, "We've met."

James Ferguson, called Jamie, by his few friends, wearing a tartan jacket, brown corduroy pants, sand colored desert boots stood out dramatically against the other conservatively dressed male guests. His wife dressed in simple blue dress emphasizing her corpulent figure, both speaking with a soft Scottish burr, both looking decidedly out of place. Ferguson, employed in the British civil service, emigrated to Canada joining the federal public service, fighting and clawing his way up to his present position by sheer determination and ruthlessness. It often said, "No one should turn his back on Jamie Ferguson!"

Aware of Ferguson's groundless animosity towards Muldoon, Scott kept the two couples at opposite ends of the living room. Ferguson didn't mind, standing near the make-shift bar enabled him regularly refilling his glass.

Scott, speaking with one of the other couples excused himself seeing Carole motioning to him from across the room, George Arnott, the Deputy Minister had arrived.

Ferguson seeing him enter the room with Scott, rushed over to greet him, slurring his words, "Deputy, it's good to see you."

"Ah! Yes Ferguson."Arnott replied, then turned away facing Beaumont, "Looks like a great party Scott. Where is that beautiful wife of yours?"

Ferguson touching his elbow, plaintively asked, "Mister Arnott I'd like you to meet my wife." He had left standing alone on the other side the room.

"Yes, of course, I'll meet her presently." turning back to Scott, found him waving at his wife who was speaking with Anne. Good heavens Scott, what a striking pair of women! Who is that with Carole?"

"It's Tony Muldoon's wife Anne."

"Muldoon! Isn't he the one sent to us from defense?"

"Yes, he's a good one too, Mister Arnott!"

"Good, I'd like to meet him. By the way, Scott, how is your father? I heard he isn't well?"

"Some heart problems Deputy but he's coming along."

"That's excellent. Tell the General I'll arrange a trip to visit him as soon as I finish the work assigned me by the Minister some of which you and Ferguson are working on."

"Yes, sir, I'll pass it on, he'll be very pleased to see you." Scott then ushered his Deputy to where his wife and the Muldoon's were standing, after introducing Arnott to Tony and Anne, leaving, replenishing his other guests' drinks.

Ferguson, busy drinking double scotches, collared Beaumont, "That's a beautiful grand piano you have over there, do you play?"

"No, not really Mister Ferguson, but my wife does."

"Will she play for us?"

"She'd be happy to but she has to take care of the hors d'oeuvres for our guests, we do have another player present."

"Who?"

"Tony Muldoon." Scott replied.

"Oh not that Paddy! " Ferguson drunkenly responded

Ignoring Ferguson's rudeness, Scott called over to Muldoon, in deep conversation with Mister Arnott, "Tony would you play for us?"

"Sure Scott, I'll be glad to. Excuse me Mister Arnott." As he turned to move over to the piano, the Deputy patted him on the back, a friendly gesture infuriating Ferguson, who had been watching them, resenting their friendly exchange.

Anne worriedly tugged at his arm, warning him to be careful, mixing drinks and the piano was a bad idea at an affair like this. Kissing her on the cheek, Tony assured her she had nothing to worry about, a few Irish tunes should liven things up. As Tony played. singing in a passable tenor key, Beaumont's guests gathered around him, including George Arnott, a few singing along with him.

Not James Ferguson, fuming over the attention Muldoon was receiving, snarled in a loud, alcohol punctuated voice,

"Muldoon! Must we listen to this damn Paddy music?"

Tony stopped playing, a hushed silence filled the room, Beaumont putting his hand on an irate Muldoon's shoulder, Anne visibly upset. Arnott, after looking directly at Ferguson, walked away shaking his head. The congenial mood broken, the party started breaking up. The first to leave, the Fergusons departing without saying a word. Following them George Arnott warmly shaking Scott and Tony's hands, smiling broadly after being kissed on the cheek by both Carole and Anne.

Walking to Arnott' s car, the Deputy stopped, putting an arm around Beaumont's shoulder said, "Scott, except for that unfortunate incident at the piano, it was a very good party. I'm going to meet with you shortly, there are a number of issues I want to discuss."

"Thank you sir, I'm looking forward to it."

As the Muldoon's were leaving, Scott, shaking Tony's hand, said reassuringly, "Don't let the Ferguson incident get under your skin, you're doing a fine job and the Deputy knows it." Scott, taking Anne's hand in a warm, lingering handshake, looking deeply into her eyes, his voice husky, "I'm looking forward to seeing you again, Anne."

"I hope so too, Scott." she murmured, softly.

While driving home, a grimly quiet Anne suddenly blurted,

"Why did you have to play the piano and sing those corny Irish songs?"

Shocked, Tony angrily replied, "Damn it Anne, I didn't do anything wrong! They were enjoying it, so was the Deputy. It's that damn Ferguson! He's had it in for me from the beginning., besides, Scott has assured me I have nothing to worry about." Changing the subject he asked her what she thought of the Beaumont's. She replied saying she thought them to be very nice, especially Scott who she found to be confident, self-assured, as for his wife she thought she was a cool one, very self controlled.

Arriving at their apartment, Anne felt disheartened by its comparison to the luxury of the Beaumont residence. Later, while undressing, hearing Tony humming in the bathroom, wondered when she might see Scott Beaumont again.

CHAPTER 5

Beaumont Meets With His Deputy Minister

Scott Beaumont received his call to George Arnott's comfortable office the Monday morning following the Ferguson incident at the cocktail party. On arriving he was asked to wait in the ante room as the Deputy was on the phone speaking with David Preston, the Clerk of the Privy Council and Secretary to the Cabinet. After finishing his call, came out personally ushering Beaumont into his office, seated him in a comfortable chair in the small sitting room adjoining. Pleasantly surprised, sensing this wasn't to be a usual meeting, Scott waited expectantly as Arnott seated himself in the chair opposite.

The Deputy, excusing himself for the delay, asked pointedly, "Scott, what is your honest opinion of James Ferguson?"

Pausing, Beaumont replied, "I'd rather not say Mister Arnott!"

"Splendid Scott, that's the type of response I expected from you, now to business. I've decided to assign him to other duties.

After discussing it with David Preston, he's being seconded to External Affairs to conduct a comprehensive study on Canada's overseas business promotion efforts starting to-morrow. Scott, I want you to take his place on an acting basis with no assurance at this time that it will be confirmed, Preston was adamant about this as you are relatively junior. In my opinion you're the best person for the job. Is this agreeable to you?"

Not surprised at Ferguson's speedy removal Beaumont stunned, knowing he was junior to a number of more experienced officers in the department, readily accepted, "I'm very flattered, Mister Arnott, I'll give it my very best, you can count on it!"

"I know I can Scott. You wouldn't be the General's son if I couldn't, that's why I'm appointing you!" he replied, smiling, adding, "If there is any resentment among your more senior colleagues you'll have to deal with it."

After assuring Arnott he would added quietly, "I regret the business at the house Friday night, I know Tony Muldoon regrets it too."

"Tell Muldoon he has nothing to regret, I admire his spunk!" Arnott replied emphatically,

"Quite right, sir, he's not afraid to express s frank opinion, he's been very helpful on the project."

"Ah yes, the project, I expect you keep the lead until it's dealt with by the Cabinet. Does Muldoon write well?"

Assuring Arnott that he did, Scott learned there was an opening in the department's communication division for someone who writes well, capable of preparing impressive press releases as well as speeches for the Minister, dealing effectively with the press. After assuring the Deputy he felt Tony would be ideal for the position, Arnott instructed Scott to inform Muldoon, then make the necessary arrangements with Personnel and the Public Service Commission.

Arnott stood up signaling their meeting was over extending his hand, "Good luck, Scott, give my regards to your father."

Beaumont left feeling ecstatic, not only had he received good news, he had very good news for Muldoon. Arnott on the other hand looked tired, not relishing meeting with Ferguson as well as having to deal with the concerns of his Minister over the pressure exerted by the Prime Minister for him to produce results helping to significantly reduce the increasing negative reporting by the media over the government's performance.

The Porter minority Liberal government was under relentless attack by the Conservatives, led by its energetic new leader, Grant Talbot. Even the removal of several Ministers reputed to have been involved in preferential granting of contracts as well as shuffling a few others had not helped improve the increasingly negative polling results for the Liberals. Some Ministers complained their Deputies were either too old or out of touch with conditions in an evolving Canada, wanting them replaced, bringing in younger blood with new, more progressive ideas and recommendations.

Arnott having recently turned sixty, sensed he was one his Minister would like to see retire early, recently signaled to him by Preston, not in broaching the subject, in the way he had raised it during their conversation on his intention of replacing Ferguson with Beaumont. Preston had pointed out, an influx of new blood in the higher echelons of his department might be a good thing. Arnott concluded the Secretary probably also meant him. Of more immediate concern to him was an offhand remark by Preston, of a new Minister for his department. Although asked Preston didn't say who he was, he didn't have to, Arnott aware that the PM was looking for a new portfolio for Big John Braxton, a popular vote getting Windsor politician, currently the Minister of Immigration.

CHAPTER 6

James Ferguson Meets With George Arnott

Arnott's musings were interrupted by his secretary announcing James Ferguson had arrived for their appointment. Sighing deeply, asked her to have him wait while he looked over Ferguson's personnel file placed earlier on his desk. Pensively reviewing it, reluctantly admitting, during Ferguson's years in the Public Service, his performance had been generally satisfactory. It wasn't his being incompetent, it was his overbearing attitude with subordinates and other junior officials, while sometimes painfully, obsequious with senior officers. Putting the file down asked Ferguson sent in.

On entering, not having slept the past weekend, Ferguson, looking distraught, broke into a torrent of words apologizing for his behavior at the Beaumont's, blaming it on having had too much to drink, "I'm not offering it as an excuse Deputy, I was overtired, I assure it's not the way I normally behave at such events."

"Yes James, it was unfortunate but isn't the reason I asked to see you, please sit," Arnott pointing to one of the swivel chairs in front of his desk. "The PM has requested External Affairs carry out an in depth study on our overseas trading patterns. David Preston and I feel you're ideally suited for this important task."

"Sounds like a real challenge, sir, when is it due to start?"

"Right away I'm afraid, Preston needs to know your answer by this afternoon."

"When the project is finished, will I be returning to my present position?"

"No, I don't think so, a suitable assignment will be found for you when that happens." Arnott replied.

"How about my replacement, shouldn't I spend some briefing him?"

"That won't be necessary James."

"May I ask who you have in mind?"

"Yes, of course, it's Scott Beaumont, on an acting basis, effective immediately!"

"So that's it! I get the sack and Beaumont gets my job!" Ferguson snapped rising angrily from his chair.

Arnott coldly interjected, "Sit down Ferguson, stop being a damn fool! You have two choices, accept the assignment or resign! I Strongly recommend the former, it could be an opportunity for you."

Deflated, Ferguson sat.

"I apologize Deputy, I'll take the assignment."

"Good, that's settled ." Arnott replied standing up terminating the meeting, wished Ferguson well without shaking his hand.

Arnott then called Preston confirming Ferguson's acceptance of the assignment. "Fine, that takes care of that little problem. By the way, George, you're getting a new Minister, John Braxton, the PM will be announcing it this afternoon, good luck!"

"Thanks, David, I'll need it! My briefing books will be ready for his arrival."

Returning to his office, Beaumont called Muldoon, informing him about the opening in the department's communications division and the DM saying he thought Tony would be a good fit for the job.

Dumbfounded Tony exclaimed, "You mean to tell me it was Mister Arnott himself recommending me for the job?"

"Yes Tony, it was Arnott himself! But for the life me I don't understand why? Perhaps he just likes Irish music." Scott laughingly replied.

"I still can't believe it Scott. I had one hell of a weekend, Anne hardly spoke to me certain that I would be fired, just wait until she hears the news, but what about Ferguson, surely he won't agree to it?"

"That's no longer a problem." Scott replied looking serious. "He's leaving the department for a special assignment at External starting tomorrow."

"That is good news!" Muldoon replied, his face beaming. "Whose our new boss?"

Momentarily hesitating, Scott replied, "For the moment it's going to be me on an acting basis."

"Say, that's really great! Congratulations! Now we both have something to celebrate. After I phone Anne the good news, let's toast our good fortune with a drink, I'll buy!"

"Thanks all the same, Tony, another time, I have lot to do before tomorrow. When speaking with your wife, give her Carole and my best regards, it was a pleasure meeting her, she's very attractive."

For a brief moment Muldoon experienced a pang of jealousy, recalling seeing Beaumont's arm around his wife's waist as they sang together while he played. Quickly dismissing the thought, phoned Anne the god news excitedly asking, "Are you proud of me?"

"Yes I am. I'll show you just how much when you come home!" she teased. After hanging up her phone, Anne found herself thinking about Scott Beaumont and the tingling sensation she enjoyed when he put arm around her waist, while her husband was playing.

CHAPTER 7

John Braxton

Big John Braxton wasted little time making his presence felt in his new department, still smarting from his acrimonious meeting with the Prime Minister who had made it abundantly clear, he wasn't pleased with his handling of the Immigration portfolio. He softened his criticism saying he should have given him the Industry responsibility in the first place, as it was better suited to his temperament. Finally, carefully measuring his words, cautioned Braxton to be very circumspect managing his new portfolio. The government couldn't tolerate another scandal like the conflict of interest business plaguing it in daily coverage by the media. Porter's government was reeling under daily attacks in the House by the Grant Talbot led Conservatives and the newly rejuvenated New Democratic Party under its young, dynamic leader, Jake Enright. The NDP, holding the balance of power in the House, threatening to join the Tories in defeating the Liberal minority government forcing an election.

Assuring the PM he would be a sterling example of probity and prudence in the Industry department left to be briefed by David Preston on his new responsibilities. Porter, watching Braxton leave wasn't sure he'd made a good choice.

Braxton, uncomfortable having to meet Preston, intimidated by his superior intellectual ability, his immense knowledge of government procedures. He knew Porter trusted him implicitly and aware that more than one Minister had lost his portfolio on his recommendation. Preston led him into his spacious office located a few doors away from the PM, seated him in a comfortable armchair at the end of the room. After presenting him with a folder containing notes on his portfolio, resumes of key departmental officials including George Arnott's, a rundown on the his department and its major issues. He finished by briefing him on senior personnel including recent changes, concluded with a rundown on his Deputy.

"Arnott is a very capable and intelligent senior official, has done a yeoman's job in building up the department, showing no traces of flagging despite recently turning sixty."

Looking surprised, Braxton interjected, "Sixty? That seems a little old. I thought the policy was to set fifty as a limit, the Deputy at Immigration is only forty."

"Yes Minister, that will be resolved if George decides to retire early or the PM feels a change is needed to give a younger man, more up to date on current business practices, a chance." Preston coldly replied.

Braxton felt a chill realizing his deputy's tenure, perhaps even his own, were in the hands of this dominating bureaucrat. Returning to his departmental office, Braxton poured himself a stiff drink before phoning his wife about his new appointment.

Fiona Braxton refused to live in Ottawa for reasons readily understood by her errant husband, preferring to live in her comfortable Windsor home close to her family and friends, her husband flying home on weekends to be with her and the two children from her first marriage to a newspaper publisher, as well as attending to his constituency affairs, a practice inherited from his late, unlamented father, once a powerful political ward heeler and liberal back room organizer. A shameless womanizer, Harold Braxton regularly slipped into a willing married woman's bed usually after her dutiful husband had left for work, his father's notoriety, resulting in family shouting matches his mother, often threatening to leave her husband, never did.

When only eight Braxton clearly remembered the day, shortly before his mother's death, accompanying his father visiting a friend of his mother, spending the afternoon sitting in her small living room. Tears streaming down his face, tried to block out the sounds of grunting, low moans, loud squeaking bed springs from behind her closed bedroom door, finally reaching a crescendo with her shouting, "Stop Harold... Not again! Please stop! Oh lord, you're killing me!"

That evening, while visiting his bedridden mother, dying from a terminal cancer, when she asked where he had been that afternoon, John broke into tears fleeing from her room . After his mother's death, spent most of his youth living with his financially secure grandparents. Years later, while attending University, still able to smile grimly recalling the day, called from an economics class, told his father had died in bed while entertaining a lady.

On arriving at his department with his special assistant, Cathy Wilson, Braxton's first act was meeting his Deputy, who, on arriving at the anteroom of his Minister's office, felt apprehensive at the prospect of working with his new Minister, by all reports not inclined to be open with his professional staff, often creating needless problems for his department. Squaring his shoulders, ushered into his Minister's office was greeted by a smiling Braxton rising from his chair, shaking his hand, motioning to a settee. Arnott nodded, frowning as he sat on seeing Cathy Wilson seated at the far end of the room with a note book in hand.

Noting Arnott's reaction to her presence, Braxton waved his hand at her as he sat opposite him, "Don't mind her Mister Arnott, she usually sits in when I meet with staff, it helps keep the record straight. I hope you don't mind?"

"Not at all' Minister, not at all."

Feeling uncomfortable in the presence of the immaculately groomed man seated opposite who seemed coolly appraising him. He felt shabby in his rumpled gabardine suit badly in need of a pressing. John Braxton, one of the most competent speakers in the House, sat awestruck as Arnott skillfully briefed him on the department's programs, not once referring to a note. He displayed a complete grasp of their technical, economic and political implications.

Arnott finished saying, "What I've just given you is a broad overview. At your convenience, I'll arrange for the program heads to brief you in more detail." It was an impressive performance, duly noted by Cathy Wilson.

"Thanks Mister Arnott, I would like that, especially your regional development plans for Western Ontario."

The inference was not lost by Arnott, knowing Braxton meant the Windsor area. "Of course Minister, I'll arrange for the regional branch head to meet with you. He's the Scott Beaumont I mentioned, a young very capable officer. In fact he's just completed a paper on the subject along with a publicity program highlighting its regional benefits. You may want to see it before meeting him."

"Yes Mister Arnott, I would like that, thanks."

After Arnott left Braxton asked his assistant her opinion of their new Deputy Minister.

She replied, "Well, John, he certainly knows what he's talking about, I don't think he liked me sitting in, he never once looked at me the whole time!" she replied frowning, seating herself in the chair vacated by Arnott.

"That's too damn bad, he'll have to get used to the way I do things!"he thundered. "Say kid, you look tired. How about a drink? I had my driver bring in some booze earlier today."

"Sure John, why not! It's been quite a day."

CHAPTER 8

Cathy Wilson

Cathy Wilson, born and bred in Windsor, a devoted Braxton loyalist campaign worker for nearly five years, followed him to Ottawa shortly after the break-up of her brief marriage to a Windsor high school teacher, unable to accept her time consuming involvement in local Liberal politics. Attractive, passionate, although providing him with some creature comforts during their earlier years together, both realizing there was no future in it, they stopped by mutual consent.

Slowly sipping her drink, looking at Braxton idly nursing his glass, sensing something was wrong, quietly asked, "Are you alright? Is something wrong, John? I wouldn't take to heart what the PM said to you. He needs your vote getting strength at home so stop worrying."

"No Cathy, it's not the new job. I'm thankful I still have a cabinet position, it's something else." he replied lapsing into silence. It was late, feeling he wanted to be alone, she put her half finished drink down rose to leave.

"Cathy, before you go, please ring up my broker.?"

"Which one, John?"

"Weece, Harvey Weece of Grant and Marshall."

After Cathy left to place his call, pounding his fist on the table, causing Cathy's glass to spill over, cursed himself for having borrowed so heavily from his bank, investing all of it in a 'sure thing' high tech stock suddenly plunging to half of its purchase value. The bank aware of this and his precarious financial position, demanded its money which he didn't have. Another serious concern was how the Prime Minster would react should he be made aware of his financial situation, the possible impact on the press, the public, the Opposition in the House. A bankrupt Minister of Industry wasn't an asset for a minority government fighting for its life. His intercom interrupted his dire chain of thoughts, "Is it Weece, Cathy?"

"No, it's Jack Colter from your bank, he's anxious to speak with you."

"I don't want to talk to him until I talk to Weece. Tell Colter I'm tied up and will call him later."

There was only one thing left to him to do, call up his wife, on some pretext convince her to take out a large mortgage on the home she loved, left to her by her father, it wouldn't be easy; it had to be done, his intercom lighting up again," Yes Cathy?"

"His office says he's unavailable, he's out of town."

"I'm not surprised, the dirty son of a bitch! Did he ever do a number on me. Sure thing indeed!" Picking up his phone dialed his wife, praying she would be home.

Calling it a day, Cathy went home to the centre town apartment she shared with another girl, Shirley Martin, for several years a member of the Ottawa scene, one feeling duty bound to sleep with her boss if asked. Surprised at finding her home, this being the weeknight she usually spent with her employer at his cottage near the Rideau river, asked her the reason.

Looking pained Shirley explained saying,he couldn't make because it was one of his kid's birthdays. Brightening up, suggesting, "Cathy, I have a great idea, I'll take you to the Oasis, it's great place, good food, lots of attractive men on the make and the boss, Nicky Gregorian, handsome as sin, a real charmer both in and out of bed."

"How would you know that?"

"I had a one night stand with him, it was incredible, he only wanting one night with no hard feelings."

"And you agreed?" an incredulous Cathy asked.

"Why not? Don't be so prudish, it was worth it. I'm just not his type but we get along fine. He was a hell of a lot better than the one I'm with now!"

Her interest aroused Cathy agreed saying, "Ok! I'm not interested in any action, certainly not in a one night stand."

"Great, put on something sexy. You'll love meeting Nicky."

"Come on Shirley, he can't be that good."

"That good? Look my girl, if there was such a thing as a love-making Olympics, he'd win all the gold medals!"she replied laughing.

"How did you come to meet him and why would he want to meet me?"

"For starters you're better looking than me, you're a Minister's assistant; he loves meeting Ministers like Jack."

"Jack who?"

"He's my Minister dummy!"a worldly wise Shirley explained. Asking her room- mate to pour them a drink.

Cathy left to take a shower, humming, thinking of Nicky Gregorian.

CHAPTER 9

Gregorian

Niccolo 'Nicky' Gregorian, son of Florentine parents, orphaned by their deaths in a tragic train accident while only ten, brought up by his Uncle Roberto, a prominent restaurateur in the Medici capitol, who worshipped the boy treating him like a second son. Growing up in his uncle's palatial residence across the Arno river, not far from the Pitti palace. Within walking distance, his uncle's restaurant located on the north side of the river near the Ponte Vecchio bridge, close to the Anglo-Americano hotel. A stunning looking child, Nicky, as his friends called him, developed into a handsome teenager. He was tall, slim, broad shouldered, an engaging smile, features not unnoticed by many teen aged girls as well as some women. He worked regularly in the restaurant after school and on weekends, learning the business from the ground up.

Nicky's uncle making regular business trips to Rome, Naples, Palermo, lately, Paris, often taking his nephew with him who eventually learned the main source of his Uncle's wealth wasn't the restaurant. He was a charter member of a drug Syndicate now headquartered in the Parisian capitol. This didn't bother Gregorian discovering the other members had families, entertained generously at large weekend family gatherings at their country estates. Like his Uncle, they ran legitimate businesses like the one in Paris, a prosperous cosmetics import export business ideally suited for the marketing their nefarious drug products overseas, including to Canada and the United States.

At the urging of his Uncle, now retired from the restaurant due to ill health, Nicky was spending increasingly more time in Paris, enjoying its free and easy life style, its night life and its women, young, middle-aged, older, ranging from Countesses to shop girls. Now in his middle thirties never giving any thought to marriage, enjoyed the readily available variety.

The Syndicate's head, Boris Aristine, liked the young Gregorian's style and manner keeping him primarily involved in the legitimate end of the enterprise, the import - export cosmetic business. Learning from a highly placed government informant, that the French Secret Service along with Interpol was carrying out a massive investigation of the Syndicate's operations decided moving the center of his drug sales operation to Canada, giving him direct access to the North American market.

Advised by Montreal Syndicate's legal advisor, doing this entailed gaining the support of some highly placed federal government officials at the Ministerial level, required establishing a legitimate Syndicate presence in Ottawa. As it was generally known a number of senior government officials enjoyed a good party, an attractive restaurant-bar would be a good way of doing this. After a lengthy Syndicate members' discussion decided financing such a enterprise.

Aristine was impressed by Gregorian's considerable experience in the restaurant business, stunning appearance, charming manner.

A natural linguist, Nicky learned to speak English at the urging of his uncle, practicing it on the many English speaking tourists visiting his beautiful culture laden city every year, French during his time in Paris. As a result Niccolo Gregorian was selected by Aristine for establishing a Syndicate business presence in Ottawa.

On being told, elated handed this great opportunity, but shocked, Nicky asked, "Ottawa! Where in the hell is Ottawa?"

About to leave for Canada, his first stop there meeting the Montreal Syndicate members, Aristine took him aside, cautioning him to remember, his function was to help resolve a major Syndicate problem, not create one, to take it easy with women, Ottawa isn't Paris.

Effectively supported by the resourceful Montreal Syndicate, Gregorian quickly established his presence, opening a fashionable restaurant-club in Ottawa's downtown market area, within walking distance from the Parliament buildings. Tastefully decorated and furnished, attractively lighted, a long mahogany bar fronted by comfortable swivel foot stools, a sizeable dancing area, great food and music, elaborate selection of wines and liquors, called, 'The Oasis.'

Hosting it wearing an expensive skin tight black silk suit, a black shirt, white tie and a white carnation in his lapel tall, slim, broad shouldered. carefully combed black wavy hair, Nicky Gregorian presented an imposing sight at the door. The welcomed patrons were skillfully ushered to a table or the bar by attractive short-skirted waitresses wearing black nylon stockings on their shapely legs. His club opening was a huge success receiving rave notices in the local press, not only pleasing Nicky, more importantly, the Syndicate.

In keeping with his carefully cultivated image, Gregorian drove a black corvette, rented a luxurious penthouse apartment lavishly furnished, a large king sized bed, black silk sheets and pillow cases. As they had hoped, the club's regular patrons, young affluent professionals, were soon joined by senior government officials and a few Cabinet Ministers with their wives or girl-friends. Despite Aristine's caution before leaving Paris, Nicky's bed was seldom without an attractive lady. After being opened a month, in line with the Syndicate's directions, Gregorian began hosting private parties for specially invited guests. The Paris and Montreal members impatient to see results from their large investment in the Ottawa operation increased the pressure on Gregorian.

CHAPTER 10

Cathy Meets Nicky

When Shirley Martin entered the Oasis followed by a reluctant Cathy Wilson, Gregorian was behind the bar checking stock with the head bartender, hearing them enter, turned around recognizing Shirley, not the very attractive woman hesitatingly following her. Having used Martin to meet her Minister, finding him useless for the Syndicate's, purposes, restricted himself to a single night episode she found wonderful, he, thought boring but impressed by her friendly nature and understanding. Reaching the bar with Cathy in tow Shirley was met by a smiling Gregorian, taking her hand to kiss.

Shirley pushed Cathy forward, "Nicky darling, I want you to meet a good friend of mine, Cathy Wilson, special assistant to John Braxton the new Minister of Industry formerly of Immigration."

"Really?" Taking Cathy's hesitant hand kissed it causing her to blush furiously. "It's a real pleasure meeting you Cathy. Shirley! Why have you kept this lovely creature hidden from me?"

Pulling her hand away in embarrassment haltingly replied,

"Mister Gregorian, you're a shameless flatterer." A waitress brought them a magnum of imported Champagne compliments of Mister Gregorian.

The weeks following were the happiest Cathy had ever known. As Shirley wisely predicted, she and Gregorian soon became lovers, her ardent, extremely handsome Italian sending her roses daily at the beginning spending most of his nights with her.

Her envious friend teased her relentlessly, "Come on Cathy tell me honestly how you find him in bed?"

"What a question to ask. Shirley, you know!"

"Yes, but only once, it's not the same thing, he really seems to have really gone for you, besides I think his only interest in me was to help him meet my Minister. Has he asked you about meeting your boss?"

"No, of course not, what a question!" Cathy angrily responded.

"Look, I'm only trying to be helpful I'd hate to see you being hurt, don't be surprised if he does."

Cathy blanched, remembering on the previous night Gregorian, hosting one of his private parties, suggested she invite Shirley to bring along her Minister, and Cathy inviting John Braxton. Believing her friend's insinuation ridiculous, dismissed it from her mind. The opportunity for her to do so surprisingly arose the following day.

After pouring Braxton coffee smiling he asked her, "I understand from the grape vine you're quite involved with someone?"

Embarrassed, hesitating, she replied, "Ah, Yes, I suppose you could say that, he's very nice. It's Nicky Gregorian, the owner of that new club in the Market."

"Well Cathy, I'm really impressed, he must be really loaded able to open a club I've been told is really something to see, in fact I wouldn't mind seeing it myself some time."

Wilson interrupted him, "As a matter of fact, John, he's holding a private party next Tuesday night I'm sure he would like you to attend if you're interested. You wouldn't be alone, several other Ministers plan to attend."

"In that case fine. When does it start?"

"At six for cocktails, dinner at seven thirty."

"Fine Cathy, I'll meet you there at seven."

CHAPTER 11

Braxton Meets Gregorian - The Trap

By the time Braxton and Gregorian met the night of the party, Nicky had learned a great deal about Big John Braxton from Cathy, including his financial problems, a factor of particular interest to him also learning Cathy's Minister was not averse to receiving or giving favors. In the following weeks Braxton and Gregorian appeared engaged in a friendly relationship despite their significant age difference. Nicky constantly stroked his huge ego, praising him for political accomplishments a love-struck Cathy related to him, seemingly sought the politician's advice on business matters. Braxton obviously enjoyed the younger man's company, the generous lunches and dinners, the evening entertainment, the beautiful young women Gregorian had sit at their table under Cathy's watchful eye.

After a month with the Montreal Syndicate increasing the pressure on Gregorian, he sprung his trap on Big John, saying he was about to invest heavily in a really hot reliable stock market tip, urging the hapless, cash-strapped politician to join him keeping the tip under his hat. Braxton hesitated, telling his new found friend that he'd recently been burned by a so called 'sure thing' stock market tip.

"Come on John, do think I would investing a quarter of a million dollars of my company's money in it if it wasn't?"

"No, I guess not, it's no use Nicky I don't have the money!"

"No problem John, I can arrange it for you from my principals. Do you think I would do that if it wasn't a sure thing?"

"I suppose not, how much would they be good for?"

"Oh, I'd say a hundred thousand."

Braxton enthusiastically seeing it a sure way to recoup his heavy losses including the money raised by his wife heavily mortgaging her home in Windsor, paying off his initial Ottawa bank loan replied, "Ok Nicky, let's do it!"

As promised, the money was quickly raised provided by the Syndicate's Montreal bank, used to purchase the stock recommended by Gregorian. It initially rose a few points then quickly plunged to a quarter of its purchased value. The bank wasted no time demanding its money. A distraught enraged Braxton met an apologetic Gregorian in his Oasis office shortly after the stock purchase disaster, not mollified by Nicky saying he also took a major financial bath. Offering to help Braxton in any way he could, was angrily refused by John, fearing his political career and personal life were about to collapse. Gregorian having convinced the increasingly concerned Syndicate members, Braxton's potential influence was a major step forward towards achieving their objective, Aristine's legal Canadian entry, couldn't afford to lose him. Nicky increasingly pressured Cathy to convince her boss to accept his offer of help. Braxton, now desperate, nowhere else to turn, reluctantly agreed.

When they met late one evening, wasting no time, Gregorian asked, "How can I help you John?"

"I need another hundred thousand. Can you manage that?"

"Yes, John I think so but I need a favor first."

"What kind of favor Nick?"

"I need your help to get someone into the country."

"Who?" a worried Braxton asked

"A friend of mine in Paris, Boris Aristine."

"Aristine? I know that name!" Braxton angrily replied, "It came up while I was at Immigration, he's an infamous drug dealer operating out of Paris!"

"That's never been proven in court John." regorian responded quietly.

"Small wonder, I understand any potential witnesses conveniently disappeared!"

"Come, come John, that's strictly fiction. Look, he wants to leave Europe and live quietly in Canada, starting a legitimate business similar to the one he established in Paris years ago. If you agree to help us, my friends will not only clear your debt with the Montreal bank but Kick in another hundred thousand for you after Aristine is legally in Canada."

Sweating profusely an agitated Braxton replied, "I have to think about this, Okay? I'll let you know soon."

"It has to be very soon John, I must know by tomorrow afternoon. Don't worry about how we'll carry out the transaction, it'll be as clean as a Sunday shirt."

Leaving the Oasis, Braxton felt ashamed realizing what he was being asked to do, help bring a notorious European drug dealer into Canada legally. After a sleepless night, disgusted with himself, not knowing what else to do, called Gregorian agreeing to use his influence as a Minister of the Crown to help Aristine enter Canada as a landed immigrant.

CHAPTER 12

Scott Beaumont and Anne Muldoon

S cott Beaumont quickly established himself in Ferguson's job, his natural ability, flair for management, supreme self-confidence proved him to be the most accomplished of the Assistant Deputy Ministers reporting to Arnott leading to early confirmation in his new position. Meanwhile Tony Muldoon was similarly successful in his new position in Arnott's Communications division as the department's main contact with the news media, favorably impressing the Deputy and his Minister. A very preoccupied, John Braxton, despite his personal problems, congratulated Muldoon for drafting a recent speech he gave in Windsor, favorably reported in both the local and Toronto press.

Tony and Scott saw little of each other these days except for the occasional lunch. At his wife's insistence Muldoon often invited the Beaumont's to spend an evening with them. To Anne's annoyance, were politely refused until Carole was away visiting her mother in Toronto, Beaumont eagerly accepted, apologizing he would be alone. Tony's .wife didn't mind surprising her husband, it was Scott she wanted to see, often romantically day-dreaming about him since their meeting at his home.

The evening started badly, he was delayed having to attend a late meeting with Arnott discussing the regional business plan impacting on the Windsor riding. Driving to the Muldoon's, unsettled about his Deputy's remarks about their department's future inferring he might not be around much longer, confirming the rumor David Preston was pressuring Arnott to take an early retirement. Concerned over its possible impact on him should it come to pass dismissed it instead thought of Tony's wife, how much he wanted to see her again. Having found her warm, compelling, beautiful asked himself, "What was it about Anne? What am I looking for? Love? Sexual gratification?"

Anne, upset by the delay in Scott's arrival, the hot snacks she had carefully prepared were cold, for some reason, Tony couldn't understand, blaming him. When the doorbell rang an immensely relieved Tony rushed to open the door.

A contrite Beaumont entered handing him a box of flowers along with his coat, "Terribly sorry to be so late. I was unavoidably detained by the Deputy."

"I'm not the problem Scott but you better make peace with my wife." he replied trying not to laugh.

Taking the box of flowers from Tony, Scott called to Anne in the kitchen, "My sincere apologies Mistress of the house, do I need to throw my hat into the kitchen or allowed to walk in to say hello?"

Anne, coming into the living room, saw Scott and her husband standing together smiling at her. Scott handed her the box which she eagerly opened revealing six long stemmed crimson roses,

"Oh Scott, they're beautiful!" she gushed, raising them to her face.

Tony, stunned by his wife's instant transformation addressed Beaumont saying, "You should come around here more often, you wouldn't believe the hard time I was getting before you arrived."

Anne, her eyes flashing, angrily addressed her husband, "Stop exaggerating Tony, you'll have Scott believing I'm a real shrew."

Tony interjected, "Enough small talk, let's have a drink. What's your preference Scott a martini or a man's drink scotch?"

"What are you having Anne?" Beaumont asked.

"A martini, we have a whole decanter full. There may be too much water in it, I'm afraid all the ice cubes have melted." she replied apologetically.

"Then a martini it is, a little water never hurt gin." Beaumont responded.

As Anne busied herself in the kitchen, the two men updated each other on their activities. Anne finally joined them carrying a tray of warmed over treats she had carefully prepared for the occasion. Scott stared appreciatively at her wearing a stylish peasant skirt pinched in at the middle, emphasizing her slim waist, matching blouse and shoes.

Beaumont intrigued by her pert, innocent small town look, complimented her, "That's a very attractive outfit you're wearing Anne."

Her face flushing, pleased he had noticed replied, "Oh! It's just a little something I picked up at the boutique I work in."

Tony, who hadn't joined in, "Yes Hon, you look really nice."

Scott continued, "So you work in a boutique, that's interesting, what is it called?"

"'The Fashion Place', it's on the Mall near Bank street." she replied settling down with her cocktail.

"I'm afraid I'm not one familiar with boutiques, I imagine my wife is probably aware of it." Scott said regretting bringing up his wife.

"How is Carole's mother?" Anne sweetly asked.

"Feeling much better I'm happy to say." then artfully switched the conversation to Tony who wasn't the least bit reluctant talking about himself much to his wife's visible annoyance.

The atmosphere warming up after finishing another decanter of martinis, Tony played some old standard dance music on the upright piano standing against the wall while Scott and Anne danced together. Tony didn't mind, not after all Beaumont had done for them, not even when Scott hugged her when she kissed him as he was leaving, something she had not done before not even with male friends of long standing.

The Friday following Beaumont's visit to her home, Anne, while busy at her fashion shop, arranging a selection of summer fashions on a special sales rack, sensing someone was standing behind her, turned around quickly almost bumping into a grinning Scott Beaumont.

"Surprised to see me?" he asked laughing."

"Yes, I certainly am!" She replied, visibly uncomfortable noting the quizzical look, Jane Price the shop's owner was giving them.

"I didn't mean to startle you Anne, I enjoyed myself so much at your place the other night, I felt obligated to thank you again personally as well as inviting you to have lunch with me. Will you?"

"Oh Scott, I don't really know, I shouldn't with Tony out of town with the Minister." replying nervously.

"Don't be silly, Anne, it's only a lunch. I'm sure Tony wouldn't mind." he persisted.

Pausing for a moment she replied, "Very well, just give me a minute while I powder my nose and get my coat."

Scott, taking Anne to a nearby trendy restaurant specializing in French cuisine, spent the next hour chatting with her, both obviously enjoying each other's company.

Suddenly, looking at her watch, stood up. "It's getting late, Scott, I must go. I'm a working girl, not a senior government executive!"

Helping her on with her coat, feeling his warm breath on her hair as he gently pulled it over her shoulders, startled when he turned her around facing him, "Anne, I must see you again soon, tonight!"

Turning away from him quickly, sounding desperate, "That's impossible Scott! You should know better. What about your wife and my husband?"

Moving outside sounding hurt, he replied, I'm sorry Anne, I just can't help it. I haven't been able to get you out of my mind from the first moment we met. I knew the other night when I held you in my arms while we danced, it wasn't an idle fancy, somehow feeling you felt the same about me."

Alarmed, Anne starting to protest, was stopped by Scott pleading, "Don't say anything now, just think about it, please! I'll phone you around dinner time".

Reaching the entrance to her boutique, briefly shook hands as she thanked him for lunch, pensively watched him turn and wave before quickly walking down the street.

Entering the store, taking off her coat, Anne's employer, rushed over gushing,

"Who was that gorgeous man who took you to lunch? You must tell me!"

"Scott Beaumont, a good friend of my husband, Jane." she explained nervously.

"A good friend only of Tony? That's not the way it seemed me. No, not by the way he looked at you."

"Don't be silly, Jane! He and Tony are good friends and that's all."

The rest of the afternoon, she couldn't dismiss his parting remark about contacting her, fretting over what she should say when he called.

Preparing herself a light supper, kept glancing at the kitchen clock praying it wouldn't ring that he had second thoughts, it did, it wasn't Scott who answered when she picked up the phone, it was Tony calling from Toronto, "Thank heavens", she gasped.

"Hi honey, how is everything going?" he asked cheerfully, slurring his words. Her feeling of relief turning to one of annoyance,

"You must really be working hard, I can smell your breath from here!" she snapped.

"Hey, cut it out! We finished early so I got together with some of the Toronto press boys, it's part of my job you know." he replied sounding hurt, adding, "The Minister wants me stay with him until he returns to Ottawa on Sunday. He's asked me to help set up a joint press release program with some of the Ontario government people."

"I see, take as long as you want, it's all the same to me but please try to stay sober and not make a fool of yourself".

About to tell Tony about her lunch with Scott, decided against; it could wait until he came home. She had just hung up the phone when it rang again. Mesmerized, not wanting to answer let it ring until, unable to resist its constant ringing any longer picked it up. It was Scott, pleading to let him see her. Sighing deeply she agreed demanding it was to be a short visit only for a talk, nothing more. Beaumont agreeing said he'd be over in half an hour. Going to her bedroom to change, regretting agreeing to let him visit, wondering what she had let herself in for. Staring at herself in her vanity mirror grimaced saying, "Anne Muldoon, you're crazy!" she accused the reflection. Her doorbell rang, it was Scott smiling at her.

No sooner in the door, Beaumont took her in his arms, kissing her hungrily. At first passive, not resisting, she began kissing him back, passionately. Slowly backing her towards her living room sofa, they stopped, breathing heavily, started undressing each other. Scott laying her gently on the sofa, kissing in a manner he never dared do to his prudish wife. Incredibly aroused, Anne pulled Scott on top of her, they alternately made love and dozed until just before dawn. Finally sound asleep, held each other closely against the early morning chill.

Anne awoke with a start, "Scott, wake up! It's nearly morning, you must leave before someone sees you."

"What's the rush?" he murmured sleepily, aroused again.

"No Scott, there's no time for that; you really must go."

"Alright, alright, it's one hell of a way to leave a man!"

Watching Scott gather up his clothes from the living room floor and dressing, she might have laughed, seeing her lover looking as rumpled as her husband generally was, had she not felt so ashamed. After Scott left, feeling satisfied but terribly guilty, gathered her clothes from the floor went back to bed still feeling his moist warmth inside of her, fell into a deep sleep. When she awoke a few hours later she called Jane saying she wasn't feeling well and wouldn't be in. As she listened, her employer skeptical about what she was hearing, intuitively concluded, the voice was not off a woman feeling sick but of a woman in love.

"I hope she knows what she's doing! A friend of her husband indeed!"

CHAPTER 13

The Braxton Cocktail Party

Nick Gregorian was angry and worried. He was angry at the long delay in Braxton completing his end of their agreement expediting Boris Ariistine's legal entry into Canada, worried by the Syndicate's increasing impatience over this. Cathy Wilson now hopelessly in love with Gregorian, willing to do anything he asked was acting as a go-between for the two men. Nick, not wanting to antagonize Braxton, took his frustrations out on Wilson, often leaving her in tears.

One evening in his apartment enraged at yet another delay, exploded, "What do you mean telling me he needs more time, there is no more time my people want to results starting right now. You better tell him to get something going right away or there'll be a lot of trouble for both of us! Maybe if you slept with him?"

"Oh Nicky I can't do that! That was over a long time ago Nicky. Let's make love like we did before." she pleaded.

Realizing he had gone too far, picking Cathy up, carried her into his bedroom.

John Braxton was alarmed, taken aback by the urgency in Cathy's voice relating to him Gregorian's graphic message, "He's really serious John. I'm very concerned."

"So am I, I should have known better than to get involved with that bloody Italian!" pausing, looking at her intently, continued, "So should you! Surely you must realize by now, the bastard been using us. No use complaining about it now, it's too late. Cathy, call Ben Ruskin at Immigration for me, he owes me a big favor. If anyone finds out..."his voice trailing off. Reaching for a bottle in his desk drawer, poured himself a stiff drink, offering to do the same for Cathy who refused saying tersely she had to leave.

He replied, "Suit yourself. Before you leave call Tony Muldoon regarding the speech he's drafting for me. Oh yes, invite that lover boy of yours to the cocktail party we're holding next week for the government and industry brass, he is an Ottawa businessman, it might even help getting him off my back, also the Beaumont's, Arnott can't make it."

Braxton arranged the cocktail party to be held in the banquet room of a new, centre of Ottawa hotel, sparing no expense, everything, including the drinks and buffet financed by the Canadian taxpayer. Scott, although annoyed receiving the invitation, knew it was a command performance, he was replacing his Deputy. Planning seeing Anne Muldoon that night, her husband away attending a conference with Arnott in Montreal, staying overnight, he'd make some excuse to his Minister for leaving the party early, another for his wife.

Carole Beaumont was fed up, their less than active sex life dwindling to nearly zero, when they did make love, behaved as though they were doing each other a favor. At first she blamed it on the pressures of his new job, now she wasn't sure, another woman? Impossible, not Scott. Looking forward to attending Braxton's party, Carole was upset her husband telling her they would have to leave early taking her home, returning to his office to be on stand-by in case Arnott calls seeking his help for the next day's meeting. Although skeptical, shook off her doubts, turning her thoughts to what she would wear to Braxton's cocktail party, something new she thought deciding seeing what was being featured at the place where Anne Muldoon worked, The Fashion Place, hoping to find something that would reawaken her husband's desire for her.

Arriving at the shop on the early afternoon of the day of the party was met by Jane Price, Anne busy in the back room checking on some new arrivals. The shop's owner struck by the cool, very attractive, well dressed tall, blonde woman standing in front of her. Jane held out her hand introducing herself, Carole, taking her hand did the same. Jane thinking, "Beaumont! That's the name of that gorgeous man that took Anne out to Lunch recently, the good friend of her husband."

At that moment, Anne finished in the back room entered the shop, seeing Carol standing with Jane, grew pale. Regaining control of herself Anne approached them, "Hello Carole, this is a surprise, what brings you to our humble little shop?"

"I'm looking for a little something to wear at the Minister's party tonight."

"Yes Tony told me about it also that you husband would be filling in for the Deputy. Tony's in Montreal standing by in case Mister Arnott needs any help in getting ready for his presentation at the conference tomorrow."

"Scott's been asked to stand by in the office later in the evening in case his help is needed." She replied, feeling reassured over her husband's excuse for leaving early.

Anne Muldoon was relieved, knowing the real reason why Scott was doing this, although feeling guilty, was excited at the prospect of seeing her lover again. Carole left after selecting a stylish expensive black cocktail dress accentuating her beautiful long blond hair.

The Beaumont's arrived at the hotel lounge reserved for Braxton's party, shortly after seven, it was nearly filled with guests sipping cocktails passed around by smartly dressed waiters. After a courtesy greeting with his Minister, who commented on Carole's stunning appearance, mingled with the other guests, particularly noting other government senior people, including Ben Ruskin the Minister of Immigration who had replaced Braxton and the Johnsons, Paula and her husband Craig from the Privy Council Office.

There was a hush in the room at the eye catching late arrival of Nick Gregorian and Cathy Wilson. He wearing an elegantly tailored tuxedo with a black silk shirt, white bow tie white cummerbund and a white rose in his lapel, Cathy in a beautiful red, chiffon dress. Elbowing their way through the crowded room to meet Braxton who called over Ben Ruskin standing nearby to join them, as he did the Beaumont's. Carole was stunned, never before had she seen so striking a man as this impossibly handsome, tall, perfectly proportioned, swarthy Italian who gently took her hand kissing it. Startled, she quickly pulled it back.

Smiling broadly introduced himself, "I'm Nick Gregorian and this is Cathy Wilson."

Scott's wife, glowing from his unexpected, pleasurable hand-kissing replied, I'm Carole Beaumont and this is my husband Scott." tugged at his elbow, pulling him away from the Ministers.

They chatted amiably, until Braxton called Gregorian to come with him to an adjacent empty ante room for a private talk, Cathy remaining with Ruskin while the Beaumont's sought out the Johnsons. Looking at his watch, noting it was after ten Scott turned to Carole telling her it was time for them to leave. Adamantly refusing, told him she wanted to stay longer, later taking a taxi returning home. He reluctantly agreed, knowing Anne Muldoon would be impatiently waiting for him and left.

CHAPTER 14

Carole and Nicky

Gregorian, finishing his talk with Braxton re-entered the banquet room, seeing Carole Beaumont alone without a drink, collared a waiter ordering two glasses of champagne. Approaching her, flashing his most engaging smile, asked why she was standing alone. She hesitatingly replied her husband had to go to his office on an urgent matter. About to ask her if her husband would be back to take her home the waiter arrived with the champagne he ordered, handing her a glass.

She protested weakly, "Oh no, I really shouldn't."

"And why not? Mind you it's not as good as what I serve at my place but not bad, it's only champagne." Gregorian urged.

Several glasses later, their conversation becoming animated, he asked her when her husband would be returning to drive her home, she replied he expected to be quite late.

Pleased he responded, "He must be a very dedicated public servant."

"Yes he is!" she countered defensively noting the sarcasm in his remark.

"How are planning to go home if he's not returning?"

"By taxi Mister Gregorian," she responded, sighing.

"By taxi Carole? That won't be necessary, I'll drive you home and please call me Nicky."

"Well, alright, Nicky. It's getting late I should leave now but first I must 'powder my nose."

After she left to do this, Gregorian sought out Cathy busy talking some old friends telling her he had to meet later with Braxton at his club's office to discuss the serious concerns of both of them, had a taxi available to take her back to her apartment. Dubious, having watched him and Carole Beaumont together, reluctantly agreed, feeling tired, left.

While in the rest room, Carole couldn't stop thinking about the fantastically handsome Florentine with the soft Italian accent and manner she found sensually exciting. She had heard from friends of his reputation as a womanizing Latin lover. He was providing her excitement and stimulation lacking in her life, besides she could keep it under control. Satisfied at her the mirror image left, returning to Gregorian, waiting with another glass of Champagne.

She accepted it saying, "Nicky, not another one?"

"Yes, just one more, then we'll leave. Before taking you home I want you see my club and meet some of my friends. It will interesting there by now."

"Well yes, but only for a short time."

Leaving the hotel in his black corvette convertible, drove slowly to the Oasis, with its top down, allowing the fresh air to clear their heads. Arriving at the club, enthusiastically greeted by his staff including his manager, visibly impressed by the extraordinarily beautiful tall statuesque blonde he had with him, someone he hadn't seen before. For the next hour she enjoyed herself immensely, the young vibrant crowd, superlative champagne an excellent band, dancing to music she enjoyed requested by Nicky, selections from the romantic repertoire of Frank Sinatra, Perry Como and Nat King Cole. Dancing, with Nicky, a wonderful dancer, crooning in Italian into her ear. Finally, they danced to a tango requested by Nicky, referred to by Argentines as dancing seduction, an outstanding looking pair, some dancers stopped dancing to watch them.

Finally, sitting down, telling Gregorian it was wonderful but she was tired and time for her to go home. Walking to his car, the cool air making her dizzy. Leaning on his shoulder as he gently assisted Carole into the passenger side. After sleepily giving Gregorian directions to her home, dozed off as he drove away. He didn't take her home, instead headed towards his apartment. Arriving at his parking place in the dark underground garage.

Suddenly awakening, frightened by the dark Carole angrily demanded, "Where are we? This isn't my home!"

Gregorian soothingly replied, "We're at my place. You seemed to be under the weather, I thought you might like to rest awhile before going home."

"Look either take me home or call me a taxi!"

"Please Carole! Just come up to my place for a minute. You can telephone for a taxi from there if you like, you don't need to. I'll be very happy to drive you home. What are you afraid of? We're grown people."

Briefly thinking it over she agreed, "Alright, but only for a moment, then you must take me home."

After entering his apartment Carole asked to use his phone to call home, it was past one, there was no answer, she felt relieved. After sitting on large luxurious chesterfield Gregorian offered to make her a cup of Italian coffee which she refused.

Sitting beside her said sarcastically, "Your husband must be exceptionally conscientious to work this late."

Carole, sensing what was coming, not surprised when he took her in his arms kissing her passionately, without any preliminaries, pushed her down on the chesterfield, raised the hem of her dress above her waist, pulled down her underwear removing her shoes in the process, forcing himself through her resisting fingers. At first Carole screamed, then, uttering a low moan relaxed, no longer able to control herself, matched the pulsating rhythm of his rapid thrusts. After climaxing together, they laid back, he breathless sweating profusely, she sobbing, tears streaming down her face.

Pushing him off the sofa Carole shouted, "You monster, you raped me!"

"Come, come Cara Mia, I didn't rape you, I made love to you and you enjoyed it! Now I'm going to show you what Florentine loving is all about!"

Getting up from the floor removed the rest of his clothes, completely stripping her. Carole, mesmerized by his magnificent naked physique, wanted this Italian and he knew it. Picking her up, carried her into his bedroom, pulling down the coverlet, laid her down on his black silk sheets, highlighting the beauty of her white skin and blonde tresses. Gasping at the sight of his re-aroused manliness, reached out her arms invitingly, Nicky started caressing her with his tongue.

"Stop! What are you doing down there? It isn't decent!" grabbing his head in her hands.

Looking up in a passion-thickened voice exclaimed, "How do you know that? Are you telling me you never had man tongue love all of you before?"

"No, of course not! Not even my husband and stop using that disgusting expression!"

"I'm not surprised Carole. Good! Then I will be your first."

This time there was no resistance, she was ecstatic, never in her wildest imagination believed love-making could be like this.

After she climaxed, he moved up beside her, whispering hoarsely, "Cara Mia, now it's your turn."

"Yes my darling, my turn." she murmured, passionately.

Later, relaxing in the arms of her sleeping lover, sighed saying to herself, "Now I know what Florentine loving is all about!"

Carole fell into a blissful, contented sleep, her head nestled on Nicky's chest. Gregorian had succeeded in opening the Pandora's box of her hidden emotions, let her sexual Genie out of the bottle, releasing a host of deeply seated feelings, desires she never knew existed in her inner being.

For Niccolo, it was like Beatrice and Dante beside a bridge by the river Arno in his beloved Florence. In his mind, she could have been painted by Leonardo De Vinci. Michael Angelo, Raphael, for both lovers, an extract out of the biblical Song Of Songs.

Gregorian brought Carole home shortly after two am, relieved discovering her husband hadn't returned. Taking her in his arms, kissing her gently, urgently demanded, "I must be with you again, soon!"

"Of course, my darling, when?"

"Soon Cara Mia, very soon. I'll be in touch."

After watching him drive away, she entered the house, quickly undressed, bathed, went to bed falling asleep, with a mischievous smile.

Meanwhile her husband was lying beside Anne Muldoon, sound asleep. She was wide awake, consumed by guilt, not wanting to hurt her husband, falling in love with Scott, not knowing what to do. Listening to his heavy breathing lifting her head, kissed him on the forehead, murmured, "What on earth am I going to do about you?" Sighing deeply, nestled her head on his shoulder.

On arriving home shortly after five, Scott, thankful finding his wife sound asleep, quickly undressed, climbed into bed without disturbing her, falling asleep until rudely awakened by their radio alarm. Later at breakfast, both looking tired, little was said about the previous night. He using the weak excuse of falling asleep at the office. When asked by her husband how she had spent the rest of the evening Carole replied that Nick Gregorian had invited her and a few others to visit his club then drove her home. For the moment it suited both of them to live their own private lives until Tony Muldoon painfully discovered his wife's relationship with Scott Beaumont.

CHAPTER 15

Heartbreak - The Broken Dream

Tony's plan to surprise his wife with tickets to her favorite ballet, Giselle, on the Friday night of her upcoming birthday ended, his Minister requesting him to take care of the publicity aspects of the North Bay dedication of a new Federal Regional Development government building on the same day. He was surprised at her understanding acceptance of this, even though it could result in his not returning until the following Sunday. Saying she understood, would miss him, they could make up for it when he returned.

The night before his departure, in their bedroom talking as Tony packed his flight bag, a replica of his Air Force days, Anne became quiet, frowning, irritable during dinner, her husband attributing it to his missing her birthday. Putting an arm around her shoulder to comfort her, found his wife unusually stiff and unyielding.

Telling Anne how sorry he felt, that all was not lost, knelt down reaching under their bed retrieved a long box, still on his knees presented it to her saying, "Maybe this will help a little."

Giving her husband a strange look stood, holding the box tightly.

"Well open it!" he demanded.

Sitting on the edge of the bed she slowly opened the box revealing a dozen long stemmed red roses similar to those she had received from Scott.

"They're beautiful Tony, thank you." she said quietly, feeling guilty over her upcoming tryst with Scott after her husband left on the North Bay trip.

Hurt by her weak response asked her to locate the card he had included, asking her to read it out loud.

Looking down at him Anne read, "For someone as lovely as you, only a dozen roses will do." Bending over Anne kissed her kneeling husband on his cheek, "You're quite a poet Mister Muldoon ." If Anne understood the veiled reference he made to the half dozen roses given to her by Scott Beaumont, she didn't show it .

Seeing she was frowning again Tony quietly asked, "Anything wrong dear? It's rotten luck my having to be away on your birthday, I didn't have any choice." Later in bed, trying to make love to her, Anne resisted, kissing him on the forehead saying, she was tired, they could wait until his return. Concerned over her recent, decreasing interest in his love-making, Tony fell into a fitful sleep.

The next morning on arriving at the office with his flight bag, learned that the North Bay building dedication ceremony had been delayed for a week. Overjoyed phoned Anne at home from his office to give her the good news, getting no answer tried the boutique, Jane telling him she wasn't expecting Anne in that day as it was her birthday, deciding she probably had an early appointment with her hairdresser afterwards probably shopping, went on with his work.

At noon he decided to have lunch at a small local hotel known for its draft beer, pork hocks and transient airline stewardesses. After lunch, idly nursing a beer, looking into the lobby, saw a woman remarkably resembling his wife, heading towards a bank of elevators. Hesitating, believing he must be mistaken, watched her enter one, its door closing as she turned around before he could see her face. Feeling foolish, convinced his mind was working overtime, ordered a scotch and a beer chaser. Deciding to call home again, used one of the hotel's pay telephones located nearby, still no answer, now worried feeling she should be home by now. The woman he thought resembled Anne clouding his mind, deciding to wait, moved to a table giving him an unobstructed view of the elevators.

Overwhelmed by fear and jealousy asked himself "My God! Could that have been Anne after all?" Bitterly answered two hours later when his world fell apart, seeing his wife exit from an elevator closely followed by Scott Beaumont, who, looking quickly around not seeing anyone, kissed her quickly on the cheek, headed for the desk, she to the exit to the hotel parking lot.

Stunned, enraged, Muldoon's first impulse was to confront Beaumont and beat the hell out of him, deciding that could wait, followed his wife, catching up with her by their car fumbling in her purse for her keys. Seeing a grim looking Tony rapidly approaching, dropped her purse, spilling its contents all over the oil stained asphalt.

Kneeling, picking up her purse's contents, was grabbed by the shoulders and roughly pulled to her feet, her enraged husband shaking her violently, hitting her back against the car door, shouting, "You whore! You dirty Beaumont whore! Too tired for me but not too tired for him you rotten Beaumont bitch!" Muldoon in a blind fury, slapping his sobbing wife violently across her tear-stained face.

Grabbing the purse from her shaking hands, quickly picked its contents up putting them in it except for the car keys, opening a rear door throwing it into the back seat. "Get in damn you!" he growled at his wordless wife, after opening the driver side door pushing her over the transmission hump tearing her stockings.

Wordlessly driving home, furtively looking at his wife, seeing her suddenly small and helpless, bent over, sobbing, her face in her hands, her whole body shaking uncontrollably. Looking away, staring straight ahead as he drove, wanting to scream but couldn't, finally finding his voice shouted, "I'm going to kill that bastard! I should kill you too, you deceiving bitch!"

Anne stopped sobbing staring fearfully at her husband.

Arriving home, she went immediately to their bedroom closing the door. He stood in the centre of the living room, shaking, wanting to break every stick of furniture in the room. Instead he grabbed the roses out of the vase Anne had placed them in, their thorns cutting into the palms of his hands, stormed into their bedroom, threw them at her as she raised herself from their bed, he shrieked, "Happy birthday you rotten little whore!"

Storming out of the room crying, threw himself on their sofa, physically and mentally exhausted, fell into a disturbed sleep.

Still dark when he awoke early next morning, looking stupidly at his blood-stained hands, remembering what had happened, felt sick to his stomach. Cleaning himself up, went to a nearby restaurant for a morning coffee, leaving later for the Press Club where he spent the day drinking alone. Although only n honorary member, and against the rules, the manager sympathetically let him spend the night sleeping on a sofa in the lounge.

Anne was making coffee when Tony arrived home shortly after seven the next morning. Looking at him briefly, as he sat down at the kitchen table, she wearily poured him a cup of coffee handing it to him in an automatic reflex. Muldoon unshaven, bleary eyed was shocked by his wife's appearance, her face badly swollen from the hard slapping he had administrated in the parking lot, her eyes red and puffy, the painful way she was moving around the kitchen. her back hurting from his ramming it against the car door. Indescribably ashamed, he tried to speak, couldn't, never having raised his hand against her, despising men who physically abused women. Now here he was, smelling of stale sweat and alcohol, a wife beater!

Half rising from his chair, rasped, "I'd better take you to the hospital emergency."

"Stay where you are! you're not taking me anywhere!" she countered, leaving the kitchen for the bedroom slamming the door.

Muldoon began crying, his chest heaving, finally stopping, angry at his loss of self control, brow beating his wife when it was Scott Beaumont he should be after. He decided that was exactly what he was going to do. Tony not wanting his wife hear him phone Beaumont, left the apartment, driving to a nearby shopping plaza, used one of its pay phones. Dialing Scott's number waited as the phone on the other end kept ringing' about to hang up a voice answered, it was Carole, "Hello I'd like to speak to Scott." he asked, keeping his voice calm.

"Who is speaking please?" she replied, cool, detached.

"Tony, Tony Muldoon!" he answered impatiently.

"Oh! He's not here."

Knowing from the tone of her voice she was lying, not in the mood to be put off, angrily demanded, "Look Carole, I know he's there, if he knows what is good for him, he'd better come to the phone."

After an awkward pause she replied, sounding concerned, "Hold on, I'll get him."

Beaumont picked up the phone, angry, " What do you mean talking to my wife like that, she's very upset!"

Shouting, Tony replied, "Your wife's upset? You son of a bitch, you've got a bloody nerve saying that after what you've been doing with mine! I saw the two of you yesterday afternoon coming out of an elevator at the Chelsea Arms!"

Pausing, Beaumont replied in a cold flat tone, "We shouldn't be discussing this over the phone. Let's meet tomorrow and discuss it in a civilized manner."

Even though hating the bastard, Muldoon marveled at Beaumont's self-control. "No! I want to meet you now, not tomorrow."

"That's not possible, I..."

Muldoon, stopping Scott in mid-sentence, warned, "Look Beaumont, you either meet me now or I'll have a word with you wife."

"You wouldn't dare!"

"Try me!" Muldoon replied receiving some satisfaction, noting anxiety in Beaumont's tone.

"Alright! Where? When?" Naming a small park they both knew, Tony replied, in an hour.

After putting down the phone Scott saw his wife watching him intently, saying nothing.

Muldoon arrived at the empty park first, sat on a bench staring morosely at his feet, not certain what he would say to Beaumont, trying desperately to keep the angry hate of his former friend under control, when, looking up saw Scott, his jaw set, his face grim, striding towards him. Tony stood up waiting, clenching his fists by his sides.

Seeing this, Beaumont stopped short, "Look Muldoon, if it's a fight you looking for, forget it! It won't help anything. Look, I'm terribly sorry it happened, we never intended it to go that far, it just happened that's all. I promise you it won't happen again."

"Really? Does your wife know about this? How many times have you screwed mine?"

Taken aback, his eyes blazing, "Is that really important?"

"You're damn right it is! How many times?" Muldoon demanded.

Shifting uncomfortably from one foot to the other, Scott quietly replied, "We've been together three, no, four times. Look, I don't see any point continuing this conversation; it's only painful for both of us. I'm sorry..."

Tony cut in, "So you're sorry! You've said that several times, it doesn't help, how will your wife feel if she learns about this? Or is she used to it."

Beaumont's eyes narrowed, his fists tightly clenched by his sides. Muldoon stood still, praying Scott would take a swing at him giving him an excuse to punch him out.

Instead in control of himself Scott replied in a carefully measured tone, "Do you really think it helps hurting another person? Hasn't there been enough harm done already?"

Ignoring Beaumont's response Tony asked, "Is Anne in love with you? Do you love her?"

"As for the first question, you'll have to ask her, the second, No! Although I find her very attractive and charming, I don't love her."

Muldoon stood there, speechless, not knowing what to do next.

Sensing his confusion, Beaumont continued, "I'm not stupid enough to believe anything I say to you at this moment will make you feel any better. Your wife and I made a foolish mistake probably more my fault than hers. It seems she thought, perhaps foolishly, I could give her something she found missing in her life, you deserve more than an apology. Come home with me and I'll tell my wife all about this tragic business in your presence. It's your right!"

"No, nothing will be gained hurting someone else. It's your conscience you'll have to live with for what you've done with my wife, destroying my trust in you, our friendship. I warn you, Beaumont, stay away from her or I promise to Almighty God, I'll kill you!"

As Tony turned to leave, Scott made a half-hearted attempt to shake hands with him.

Muldoon turned back facing him, putting as much contempt in his voice as he could muster, "You can't be serious to think I would shake the hand of the likes of you. No, I won't tell your wife, I couldn't fall that low but I'll get even with you some day. You can bank on that!"

Unable to control his emotions any longer, Muldoon turned away walking quickly down the path to his parked car, leaving Beaumont staring at the ground. Muldoon, consumed by angry regret, sped home, tears streaming down his cheeks, pounding his steering wheel with both hands, shouting at the top of his voice, "What in God's name was wrong with me? Why didn't I punch the bastard when I had the chance?"

Arriving home found Anne sitting on their sofa, writing in a note pad on her lap, two packed suitcases at her feet, hearing Tony enter, looking up at him, "I'm just writing a note, Tony, I'm leaving you! I phoned my mother, she's agreed to let me stay with her. I'm catching the one thirty express to Toronto.".

"Is that all? What about dear loving Scott Beaumont, how can you bear to leave him?" he snarled kicking over one of suitcases, continuing, "Before you go, tell me, did you enjoy it? Was he better in bed than me?"

Her face pale, the red welt on her cheek livid, "Is that all you can say at a time like this? I'm so ashamed and sorry. I never intended to hurt you, Tony, it just happened."

"Yes, your boyfriend said the same thing. He..."

Alarmed, she cut in, "You spoke to him?"

"Yes, I'm just back. He also told me how sorry he was. Let's not change the subject, what was it like with him, seventh heaven?" he demanded his voice dripping with sarcasm, raising his hand as if to slap her.

She stood back, "Is the big man going to hit a defenseless woman again? Is that what you did to Scott?"

Her last remark made him wince, despising himself for not hitting Beaumont. Wanting to say something to hurt her instead asked softly, "Do you love him ?"

Hesitating, averting his eyes replied in a low voice, "I don't know; I'm not certain, he's so self-assured, exciting to be with but love him? I don't really know. I think...."

"Stop it, for God's sake stop it!" he pleaded, now wanting to hurt her continued, "Well, he doesn't love you, he told me so."

Looking as if Tony had slapped her again, "You're lying, he'd never say that!"

"He sure as hell did. Why don't you call him and ask him, or maybe his wife."

Raising a fist as if to strike him stopped, her shoulders drooping, her eyes downcast, raised her hands in a helpless gesture murmuring, "Oh Tony, I'm so sorry, there's nothing else for me to say."

"Yes, everybody's sorry!" He replied his voice quavering.

He impulsively wanted to push her back on the sofa, making passionate love to her hoping to erase Beaumont out of her mind realizing this would be unlikely instead, straightened the suitcase he'd kicked over, offering to drive her to the terminal which she coldly refused.

"No! I've ordered a taxi, it should be here any time now." Having no sooner spoken, the taxi arrived. Tony followed her to the taxi carrying her luggage in complete silence, watching it disappear down the street.

Looking up at the windows of his empty apartment shaking his head, exclaimed, "What in the hell am I going to do now?"

CHAPTER 16

Father Tim Crowley

As the weeks went by, Muldoon, bitterly regretting his treatment of Anne, finding her absence unbearable began drinking heavily, trying other women in a few one-night-stands in a pitiful attempt to reassure himself of his sexual ability. He failed miserably trying to wipe out his shame, his humiliation, over the hotel parking lot incident. Desperately missing his wife, realizing he still loved her despite everything, Tony wanting her back, decided calling her mother's home in Toronto. When he called, her mother answered seemingly understanding when she spoke, indicating Anne probably made her aware of the whole story prompting their marriage breakup. After telling her how badly he felt over his unpardonable behavior towards her daughter, asked to speak to Anne. Her mother sounding conciliatory, suggested she first have a chance to speak with her daughter, calling back in a few days which he agreed to do.

On his part, he had a lot of thinking to do regarding the possibility of Anne's return. Would it be possible for him to forgive and forget, when almost nightly couldn't stop imagining she and Scott together, in a Chelsea Arms hotel room? Realizing it wouldn't work unless he was able to, but how? Suddenly inspired, he'd look up Father Tim Crowley, he and Anne known him when Tony was an instructor at the Royal Canadian Air Force Navigation School. Father Tim, the base's Catholic chaplain, recently retired, becoming the Pastor of a small church in a village north of Ottawa. Checking with the Ottawa diocese office, obtained his number and called.

Father Crowley was very pleased hearing from Muldoon immediately inviting him to visit the following day, enjoying a lunch of his famous Irish stew, which Tony gratefully accepted. He found the church without difficulty after short hour drive, a small structure sporting an out of proportion bell tower, the dominant building in the village. When he drove up to the small modest attached bungalow, found a smiling Father Crowley standing in the doorway smoking his pipe He greeted his old friend with a vice like grip.

Noting Muldoon looking up at the spire, "No wise cracks, Tony, think of it as a finger pointing up to God, seeking help for all us poor mortals."

Rubbing his hand Muldoon replied, "Padre, still arm twisting ever man in sight?"

"Only the devil my boy, only the devil. It's not hard to keep in shape out here, splitting wood for the fireplace, caring for my large vegetable garden, repairs to this old cottage, keeps me busy after hours. But what about you, Tony, still fleecing beer money out of the uninformed with your one armed push- ups?"

"No Padre, but I can still take care of myself." Following his grey haired, grizzled host into the bungalow noting he was wearing his white collar and black cassock, asked, "Do you wear that all the time?"

"Not at all, usually blue jeans and a plaid shirt, a young couple wanting to get married, visited me this morning so I thought I should dress for the part."

Noting Tony wincing at the mention of the young visitors intuitively asked, "What brings you all the way out here, not just my good looks and Irish stew? And how is your lovely wife?"

The look on his visitor's face, at the mention of his wife, dramatically answered his question, his friend's marriage was in trouble. "Tony, you look like you could use a drink. My stew is simmering on the stove, we'll eat right after we finish. Now, what will you have? If you say rye you're in luck, anything else, tough."

While enjoying their drinks reminiscing about their Air Force days, the sweet aroma of the stew reminding Muldoon of his mother, finally moving to the kitchen for a generous serving of Father Tim's classic stew as well as another drink. After finishing, moved back into the living room seating themselves at each end of the fireplace.

The padre thoughtfully lighting his pipe, looking at Tony quietly asked, "Now Tony, tell me why you came all this way to see me, I'm sure it wasn't only for my stew and good looks".

During the next hour told his friend the whole story, leaving nothing out, at times choking with emotion, finishing, his voice firmer, "What really hurts, what I can't forgive myself for is the way I hit her in the parking lot, the filthy names I called her. Oh Padre, I'm so ashamed! I have never hit a woman before in my life and despised men who did! Now I'm one of them." he finished, sobbing.

After Muldoon calmed down, Father Tim, looking his friend straight in the eye, asked " Tony, you say you still love Anne, can you forgive her?"

"I don't know Padre, sometimes I think I can but when I think of her in that man 's arms I go crazy!"

"Has this ever happened before?"

"No, I don't think so. No, absolutely not!"

"How about you Tony, have you always been faithful to her?"

"No, but that's different, I didn't fall in love with any of them, they didn't mean anything to me, I didn't make a habit of it."

"So she falls out of the tree once and you want her to have a life sentence. but not you. My friend, you say you still love your wife and want her back, then don't be a stupid fool, ask her to come back, but I warn you, if you do, be prepared to fully forgive her, putting the whole tragic business behind you, man enough to ask her forgiveness for your treatment of her. It might surprise you to know, Tony, your experience though unfortunate is not unusual. From what you've told me and what I know of Anne, she's not the promiscuous type, she had a temporary lapse. I'm not going to lecture you on forgiveness, when you've been a priest as long as I have, you've heard about nearly every situation that can take place in the human condition. Believe me you situation is not unusual, only unfortunate, more important it's repairable, if you truly want it to be."

"What about if she doesn't love me anymore, wanting someone else? If she really loves me why would she go to bed with someone else?" Tony replied, angrily.

"I see, it's the sex business that has you all upset, your manly pride is bent. I recommend you look up a bible reading in Corinthians one chapter three where Saint Paul speaks of love, in it he in effect says love doesn't keep score of rights and wrongs. Tony, you must do no less if you want to save you marriage."

Nodding in silent agreement, Muldoon changed the subject to past shared experiences, an hour and several drinks later thanked Father Tim for his hospitality, his understanding.

As he was leaving, warmly shaking hands with his host heard

him say, "I hope with all my heart all goes well with you and Anne, I'll be praying for you, it wouldn't do any harm if you did some praying too. Don't be afraid to ask for God's help, he's always listening."

While driving back to the city, taking the Padre's advice to heart, Muldoon actually started praying for the first time in years. He loved his wife, wanted her back but, would she come? He had to find out deciding to call her as soon as he reached his apartment. Reaching home shortly after six, made himself a light supper, opened a beer, watched the end of the television news, phoning Toronto at seven, after ringing a number of times, about to hang up, heard the click of the phone on the other end, his heart skipped beat hearing Anne's voice, " Hello Anne, it's Tony!"

His wife replied, her voice guarded, distant, "Hello Tony, my mother told me you'd be calling, how have you been?"'

The phone shaking in his hand, overcome hearing her voice after so many weeks of separation, his voice strained, replied, "I'm OK, busy with the Minister but fine, how about you"

"I've kept myself busy helping mother. reading. thinking." Anne replied her tone cool, impersonal. Muldoon remained silent, concerned about her last comment, "Thinking about what?" he asked himself, "Scott?"

"Tony, are you still there?" her voice concerned over his silence.

"Yes, of course. By the way, I had lunch with Father Tim yesterday, he recently retired from the Air Force taking over a church in a village north of Ottawa, we had quite a talk."

Anne immediately reacted, sensing what their talk was about, "Oh, you went to see Father Tim, how is he?"

"He looks good, still making the best Irish stew I've tasted since my mother died, he asked about you."

Her voice hardened, asking, "What did you tell him?"

"The whole story, including my unforgivable behavior in the parking lot and later at home. Look Anne I can't say anything more on the phone, I must see you, will you let me speak to you if I come to Toronto?"

"I don't know, Tony. I'm not..."

"Please, we need to talk!" he pleaded.

After briefly speaking with her mother in the background, Anne replied, "Yes, f course I'll see you, when?"

"Tomorrow, I'll leave first thing in the morning and should be at your mother's by noon if that's alright with you?"

She paused, putting the phone down, calling her mother, shortly after replied, "That will be fine, mother will prepare a lunch for us."

"Great! See you around noon tomorrow, good bye." almost adding dear, choked the word off.

Muldoon, arriving at Missis Burns comfortable home the following day, met at the door by Anne's mother, dressed to go out, ushering him into her living room, calling to her daughter, waiting in her bedroom down the hall, composing herself before meeting her husband, still mentally hurting from their encounter in Ottawa.

"Anne, Tony's here. I'm on my way to meet Pricilla, your sandwiches are in the fridge and the soup simmering on the stove."

"Fine, will you talk with him for a minute? I'll be right there."

Waiting for Anne, their conversation was pleasant, encouraging, hearing Anne coming down the hall they stood up, her mother impulsively grabbing Tony's hand, whispering cautioned him, "Tony, be gentle, Anne feels terrible about what's happened, I believe in her heart she truly loves you."

Squeezing her hand affectionately, he replied, "Don't worry I will."

Nodding, she smiled as her daughter entered the room, then left them alone.

Momentarily staring at each other, awkwardly shaking hands, both laughing nervously at the unusual formality, she briefly left for the kitchen, returning with a tray carrying the soup and sandwiches her mother had thoughtfully prepared for them placing it on a coffee table.

As they sat down she spoke, "You look tired, Tony."

"You look tired too," noticing the dark circles under her eyes.

Laughing nervously, she replied, "The past weeks haven't been the best in my life"

"Mine neither." he said softly.

His wife's eyes never left his face as he recounted his talk with Father Crowley, finishing, saying,

"It's Father Tim's view, if there's any possible hope saving our marriage we should do so, before you answer, I must know, do you love Scott Beaumont?"

Turning her head away, sighing, looked back at her husband, "To be perfectly honest, at first I thought I did but after you spoke to him, he cut me off completely. Oh Tony, I feel so humiliated, so used, on top of it all, losing you. What can I say? I'm so terribly sorry, I know I can't expect you to forgive me!" Sobbing covered her tear-stained with her hands.

Moving over beside her, putting an arm around her shaking shoulders, "Anne dear, that was the very point Father Tim made, forgiveness."

"Tony, do you honestly think you can forgive me?"

"Yes! Can you forgive me for what I did to you?"

"Yes, of course, I probably deserved it."

"No Anne dear, no woman deserves to be treated like that. Now I want you to be completely honest about this, do you love me?"

"Oh yes! These past weeks I've missed you so! I realize now, instead of stupidly comparing you to Scott, I should have compared him to you, your strengths, your loving reliability, qualities he lacks but very important to me."

Although wincing at her mention of Beaumont's name, cleared her tears with a serviette, kissing her tenderly, "I want you to come home with me."

Pulling away from him, she anxiously asked, "How can I believe you honestly forgive me and not throw it in my face every time we disagree? Maybe we should wait just to be sure, we could never be happy if that starts to happen."

"Father Tim was very pointed about that, to forgive is also to forget. I promise faithfully, I'll never raise the matter again unless you give me a very good reason to do so."

On returning, Anne's mother couldn't conceal her delight seeing them in each other's arms, deciding to return to Ottawa together. On the night of their return home, as Anne lay contentedly asleep beside him, a dark thought still clouded his mind, forgiving Anne was one thing, forgiving Scott Beaumont was another.

CHAPTER 17

Reconciliation

Following their reconciliation, the Muldoon's life together assumed a new, in many ways a better direction becoming significantly more considerate of each other's moods and feelings. Beaumont's name although never mentioned at home, it was impossible for Tony not to hear or read something about him. While Tony was kept busy by both his Minister and Deputy, Anne was occupied in the boutique under Jane's watchful eye.

The Prime Minister, Donald Porter, tired of having to court the support of the Enright New Democrats keeping his minority government in power. Hoping to catch the Talbot Conservatives off balance, against the advice of some of his Ministers, including John Braxton, decided to request the approval of the Governor General to dissolve the House, calling for a General Election. Despite the political risk, the Prime Minister believed he had enough support in Ontario and Quebec to form a majority government. Muldoon had little time to think about Beaumont or anyone else, except his wife, determined to make their marriage work. Busier than ever, he drafted speeches for Braxton and accompanied him on regular vote getting forays in the Windsor area. Reluctant to leave his wife alone, he was immensely relieved by Anne's mother visiting Ottawa, shrewdly providing her daughter company on those occasions Tony had to be absent for more than a few days.

As part of their new life style, the Muldoon's made it a rule to go out, at least once a week, usually on a Saturday night, to see a film, play, occasionally, to a club for dinner and dancing. One night, decided trying the Oasis, the recently opened restaurant club, receiving rave reviews as the place to go in town. By the time they arrived, it was crowded with diners and dancers, after a short wait ushered to a table close to the kitchen entrance, waiters streaming back and forth carrying full or empty trays. After a few dances they sat, ordered their dinners, trying to enjoy the scandalously overpriced drinks, watching the gyrating antics of the dancers. Tony recognized someone he knew, Cathy Wilson, held tightly in the arms of a tall, handsome, olive colored skinned partner.

Nudging his wife, pointed them out to her, "See that couple dancing over there? The girl is Cathy Wilson, the Minister's assistant."

Anne looked at the couple not noticing the woman but the muscular athletic looking man in a skin tight black silk suit, a black silk shirt open almost to his navel, with a large gold chain around his neck, a white gardenia in his jacket lapel. Catching herself, dismissed the man from her mind, turning to her husband asked, "Isn't she the one you told me doesn't date? She sure doesn't look like that now. If they danced any closer they'd share the same skin. Speaking of skin, have you ever seen so much bare skin on a dance floor ?"

"You're beginning to show you age, dear. He probably wants to show off his hairy chest, and the gold chain."

When the music stopped, the couples leaving the dance floor, Cathy spotting Tony, brought her smiling partner over to his table,

"What a surprise, Tony, I never expected to see you in a place like this? By the way, how's your friend Scott, I haven't seen him since his move to the Privy Council?"

Bristling at the mention of Beaumont's name Muldoon replied, "I don't know, I haven't seen him for some time." Turning to his wife, white-faced by the mentioning of Beaumont's name, "This is my wife Anne."

Anne looked sharply at Wilson, with one of those artificial smiles women often give each other added "Yes, I'm the wife."

Looking quizzically at Anne, tugged at the arm of her swarthy companion introducing him, "I'd like you to meet Nick Gregorian, the owner of the Oasis."

Gregorian, after extending his hand to Tony for a firm hand shake, gently took Anne's hand, raised it to his lips kissing it, making her flush, annoying her husband, upset at the inviting way the Florentine looked at his wife while kissing her hand. On learning from Cathy Tony worked closely with Braxton, invited them to his reserved table as his guests. Although not wanting to, the temptation of a free night out at the Oasis proved too strong, Muldoon agreed. Their initial conversation was innocuous enough until Cathy asked Anne if she knew Carole Beaumont, creating a tense moment for Muldoon and his wife. Gregorian, relieved the tension ordering a round of drinks as well as a bottle of champagne After a second round, the Oasis owner casually questioned Muldoon about Braxton, finding his guest non-committal, evasive, rapidly concluded Tony either didn't know or wouldn't tell. Saying he had to attend to business, left them in Cathy Wilson's company.

Later driving home, Anne commented, "Cathy seemed quite nice, she' older than Nick I think."

Laughing, Tony replied, Yes probably a whole three or four years. In any case, he must be loaded or his family is, setting up the Oasis must have cost a fortune."

"I thought he made a passing reference to having partners?"

"Yes he did, he didn't say who they were."Tony replied.

CHAPTER 18

A New Beginning

The following Friday Braxton called Muldoon into his office informing him the man he'd replaced, Gerry Hoffer, having fully recovered, would be returning to the job as his press aid on Monday. After telling him how much he'd appreciated Tony's excellent performance in the role said, "Between these two walls, Tony, although I would have preferred to keep you on, Gerry represents important political interests in my riding, his support very important in the coming election. However I certainly could use your help with my speeches. After the election we'll see what can be done for you."

Depressed, Muldoon made his way to the Press Club for one his ritual Friday night double scotches. He was sitting alone, nursing an empty glass, when Phil Donner, a leading columnist with the Ottawa Tribune, arrived

Donner pulled up a chair beside him saying, "How's the world treating you these days, Tony?"

"Not bad. It could be worse." Muldoon replied shrugging his shoulders."

"I guess so. Say, I hear Gerry Hoffer will be back at his old stand soon?" Donner asked looking intently at Muldoon.

"Yes, but how did you know so soon ?"

"Let's just say, getting the news is my business." Donner replied smiling, ordering a round.

After half finishing his drink, Tony loosened up, "I knew it couldn't last forever, Phil, I hate to see it end."

"Well Tony, if it means anything to you coming from me. you were damn good, most of your writing is first class. I'm not the only one who thought so, as a matter of fact if you're interested, I'm sure the Tribune's features editor, Jack Thornton, would like to have a talk with you."

Looking at Donner sharply, Muldoon responded, "You don't say! What's he looking for, an inside reliable source? If that's the case, forget it. That's not my style."

"Good heavens, No! "Donner replied, irritated by the inference, "That's not what I meant at all! It's a real writing job with the paper for someone who understands how the government system works, you just might be the one."

"You're not serious Phil?"

"You're damn right I am Tony! Interested? If you are I'll set it up."

Tony ordered a refill, thinking about Donner's proposal as they talked about other things.

Donner stood up saying, "I have to go now, how about it?"

"Okay Phil, why not? Thanks."

"Don't mention it, I'll be in touch early next week."

Donner left threading his way through the tables beginning to fill up with the usual Friday night crowd. Shortly after, Tony left for home wondering how his wife would react to the news. Not surprisingly she was skeptical about the validity of the offer, concerned over the prospect of giving up the security working in the Public Service,

Anne asked, "Are you sure he was serious, maybe he had too much to drink?"

"No, he seemed serious enough. In any event it won't do any harm to follow it up if he calls."

"Yes Tony, if he calls." Anne replied he tone suggesting disbelief in any significant event happening at the Press watering hole on a Friday.

Muldoon sleeping fitfully through the night, realizing his future in the government seriously limited, particularly in light of his soured relationship with Beaumont, whose future prospects in the Public Service appeared unlimited. On the other hand, a job with the Tribune might be the right break providing the career sense of accomplishment he craved, lacking so far in his life. Finally falling into a deep sleep, dreamt of Scott Beaumont standing in front of him, laughing.

He awoke suddenly. Anne shaking him, "Tony, are you alright?"

Opening his eyes, finding her face close to his, "What's wrong?" he asked sitting up,

"You were shouting like you were in pain!" she anxiously responded.

Patting her gently on the shoulder replied, "I'm fine. I must have had a bad dream, go back to sleep."

Relieved, putting her head down on her pillow quickly falling asleep. Tony, staring at the ceiling, decided if the newspaper made him an acceptable offer, he'd go for it, perhaps then, erasing Scott Beaumont from his dreams.

Muldoon, not having heard from Donner by the end of the following Wednesday, ruefully concluded Anne had probably been right, either Donner had been pulling his leg or his editor didn't want to see him.

Arriving home, Anne met him at the door," A Phil Donner just called, isn't he the one you were talking to at the club last Friday?"

"Yes! What did he say?"

"He wants you to call right away, here, I jotted down his number."

Taking the slip of paper from her hand, kissing her on the cheek went to his phone dialing Donner's number, who, much to his relief, answered. "Hello Phil, you wanted me to call?" he asked trying to sound casual.

"Yes Tony, Jack Thornton our features editor would like to meet with you. Are you free tomorrow for lunch?"

"Yes, no problem, where and when?"

"That Italian restaurant on Metcalf at twelve thirty Don't be late he likes people to be punctual, when you get there just ask for his table, you can't miss him, he's grey haired, my height and build, smokes a large curved pipe, probably wearing a rumpled brown suit. Not to worry Tony, he knows you, seeing you at a couple of your Minister's press conferences. He was impressed by the way you handled yourself and your press release writing. I have to go now. Good luck tomorrow."

"Thanks Phil, I really appreciate this."

Putting the phone down, turned to his wife, who had been nervously listening to his side of the conversation, grabbing her by the shoulders, joyfully danced her around the room, finally stopping in front of their sofa, sat down, putting an arm around her excitedly announced, "The Tribune wants to talk to me about a possible writing job. I'm meeting the features editor, Jack Thornton, for lunch tomorrow. Darling this could be our big chance!"

"Do you really think so?" a nervous Anne worriedly asked.

"Yes, absolutely." Tony replied displaying an aura of confidence he hadn't shown for some time.

The next morning, dressing in his best suit, addressed his wife, standing behind him, "When they see me dressed like this at work, they'll probably think I'm job hunting."

"Well aren't you?" she countered frowning, apprehensive at the prospect of his giving up safe, secure employment, yet understanding why he was prepared to do it."Tony I only hope you know what you're doing?"

"Stop worrying, I won't do anything rash, it's just a lunch; it doesn't mean a job."

The morning passed agonizingly slowly for Muldoon, frequently looking at his watch, startled by Cathy Wilson's sudden appearance in his office doorway,

"Why so nervous Tony?" she asked, laughing, they having developed a friendly relationship since their meeting at the Oasis, she occasionally dropping by his office for a chat.

"It's your mind numbing allure, I always react this way in the presence of fabulous looking women." he replied good naturedly.

"The way you're dressed, I bet you're meeting one of those fabulous women today."

"No such luck, besides, where would I find a woman more attractive than you?"

"Your wife!" she shot back.

Muldoon arrived at the restaurant early, checked with the maitre d' who seated him at Thornton's reserved table. Shortly after, Jack Thornton arrived looking exactly as Phil Donner had described him.

Walking over to his table extended his hand as Tony stood up to greet him, "Hello Tony, glad you could make it." he said pleasantly shaking Muldoon's hand in a strong grip, measuring Muldoon as he did so. After ordering two double scotches, Thornton came right to the point of their meeting, "Tony, I like your work! You describe major issues clearly, Phil and other reporters tell me you're not easily intimidated. We're considering starting a column dealing mainly with the senior public service as well as local federal political issues to complement our national political coverage. I've discussed the idea in a general with our publisher, Lawrence Marsden; he likes the idea, wants to see it developed further by someone who can write, knowing both the bureaucratic and political side of the government. Although several people came to mind, Phil Donner and I think you could be the one we're looking for to develop the idea to a point demonstrating to our publisher you're the man for the job!"

Thornton paused waiting for Tony's reaction to his proposal; fortunately the waiter arrived with their drinks giving Muldoon to think it over.

After giving their order to the waiter, Thornton asked, "Well Tony, what do you think?"

Enthused by the features editor's proposal replied, "It looks like a great opportunity Mister Thornton; I'd like to give it a shot."

"Great Tony, I'm sure you won't regret it, writing for the government isn't half as challenging as writing for a real newspaper like the Tribune. By the way, call me Jack, Mister Marsden is the only one called Mister in our shop."

Extracting a sheaf of notes from his jacket inside pocket, handed them to Tony, "You'll find these notes helpful."

"When would you like me to submit my ideas?" Muldoon enquired, hoping for at least a month.

"How about a week from next Friday? We'll get together at my place in the evening."

A concerned Muldoon responding, "A week from Friday? That seems awfully short!"

Thornton brushing off Muldoon' concern, replied, "The sooner the better, Tony! I want to pursue this with the boss while he's still hot on the idea. In the newspaper business, you just don't wait for a news' opportunity, sometimes you have to create it. Tony, this is your chance!" quickly wrote his address on a serviette handing it to Muldoon.

After dinner that evening, Anne Muldoon's reservations about her husband leaving the government lessened considerably after he related to her the essence of his luncheon discussion with the Tribune editor, explaining, "There really isn't any risk. If they like what I come up with, there's a good chance of a firm offer, then we can decide. I won't make any move to resign until we have a firm offer in our hands we're happy with."

Seeming satisfied Anne replied, "Well, if that's the way it is, I don't see any harm in it." relaxing or the first time since her husband had broached the subject, kissed him warmly.

Tony spent the next two weeks working feverishly on the articles the Tribune's publisher requested submitted, receiving no direct help from either Donner or Thornton, only their encouragement, believing this was something Muldoon had to do on his own. Finally satisfied with what he had written, putting his completed articles in a large brown envelope, delivering it to Tribune one day under his deadline. Nervously waiting to learn Mister Marsden's reaction, occurring only three days after delivery. Jack Thornton, given the green light by the publisher, offered Tony a job, at a starting salary slightly under his government pay check but with possibilities for substantial increases and bonuses depending on the reader interest developed by his column.

Tony, anxious to make his mark in life, was ready to accept the challenge. His wife less enthusiastic concerned about the lower salary, giving up the generous government benefits package, the security of government employment, finding it hard accepting Jack Thornton's assurances of his certainty of her husband's success in the news world. Finally, after a long, late night discussion with her husband, Anne finally agreed. Tony accepted the Tribune's offer.

When Muldoon gave John Braxton his notice of resignation, outside of exhibiting surprise at Tony's giving up the security of a government job for a risky career in the news world, the Minister had little else to say except, liking Muldoon's work was sorry to see him leave. The Minister and his staff held a small farewell celebration for Muldoon on his last day.

Braxton smiling, taking Muldoon aside, "Well Tony, this is going to be quite a change and challenge for you, quite a responsibility as well as hazardous."

Surprised, Tony replied, "Hazardous Minister! In what way?"

"Yes, you'll have to be very circumspect about people and events especially when political bias is involved."

"Although I appreciate your advice, Minister, I won't color my articles with any political bias." Muldoon emphatically responded.

Braxton laughing, put a hand on Tony's shoulder, "That's a very noble ideal, I hope you can stick with it. Remember, the Tribune's sympathies are largely Conservative, its publisher, no friend of the government or mine! At the Tribune you won't forget you old friends will you?"

About to respond, Tony stopped, surprised seeing Cathy Wilson arriving with Nick Gregorian. Putting an arm around Tony's shoulder Braxton ushered him over where the newcomers were standing. After greeting them, Tony shaking hands with Gregorian, thanking him for his hospitality at the Oasis, Braxton, took Cathy aside telling her he wanted to have a private chat with Nick, left her with Muldoon.

Surprised by Gregorian's presence Tony commented, "I'm happy you made it Cathy but why him?" She replied, "John wanted to talk to him, that's why."

CHAPTER 19

The Tribune

Muldoon arrived early at the Tribune office on his first working day, excited at the prospect of his new job, hoping to arrive before Thornton, surprised finding the features editor waiting, welcoming him with a warm handshake. After pouring Tony a cup of strong coffee led him to his desk in the corner of the desk-cluttered news office showed him the announcement of his forthcoming column in the day's paper. In addition to briefly covering his background and government experience, emphasized his knowledge of the bureaucratic process gained while a valuable member of a Minister's staff.

Pointing to the last item, a worried Muldoon, remembering John Braxton's warning, commented, "Isn't that a bit thick, Jack?"

"Not at all, Tony, we had to underline your unique credentials not only for our readers, for our own staff. Some, who have labored long and hard for an opportunity like the one you've been given, will be watching your work closely."

"That's great! It looks like I have a couple of strikes against me before I even start?" a deeply concerned Muldoon replied.

"Not to worry, Tony, you wouldn't be here if we didn't think you could do the job. Now let's get on with it. I'll introduce you to some of our staff members, then show you how our office works." he responded encouragingly.

After a tour of the office, meeting some of the other feature writers, Tony finally sat at his desk, thumbing through one of the stack of files his editor left on his desk, looking up, surprised seeing Phil Donner heading his way stood up saying, "This is a pleasant surprise Phil, Jack Thornton told me you were on a well earned short vacation in the sun?"

"Vacations are fine Tony, I found it boring. How about you, I didn't expect our new member of the team to start until next week?"

"Yes a new member of the team thanks to you."

Jack Thornton interrupted them surprised at seeing Donner, asked them to come to his office for a briefing on Tony's first assignment, following up on rumors of bribery in government high places. He asked Donner help Tony by providing him any useful background information he had, also be the front man for Muldoon in the Press Gallery.

Leaving Thornton's office, Donner put his arm around a worried looking Muldoon's shoulder, smiling, "Not to worry Tony, it's always hard at the start, when you need any help just call me."

Sitting at his desk mulled over what he had heard from his editor about investigating rumors of bribery occurring in high places, recalled the strange relationship between John Braxton and Nick Gregorian, their closed door meeting at his retirement party. Shaking his head he dismissed it from his mind.

Muldoon's early weekly columns were a modest success, dealing with non-controversial issues such as appointments, transfers, promotions of senior and middle management public servants, created a positive response from a number of regular Tribune readers, particularly government workers. It confirmed his editor and the publisher's views that everyone likes to read gossip, especially about people in high places. He began receiving unsigned notes pertaining to unsubstantiated charges against departments, groups, individuals, alleging, favoritism in letting of contracts, promotions, transfers, towards relatives, friends, even lovers. Often included were venomous charges of racial discrimination, sex discrimination, abuse of travel and accommodation expenses. Some letters from readers outside the public service expressed a hatred, a paranoia over public servants feeding at the public trough.

After only three months, the Tribune's publisher, pleased with the reader response to Tony's Dancing around the Hill column, increased its appearance in the paper, raising his salary. As forewarned by his editor, Muldoon had to deal with the critical attitude of some of the long established columnists considering him to be no more than a political gossip columnist. This he could bear, having a regular by-line, becoming well-known, a little feared, by the Ottawa bureaucracy.

It was impossible for Muldoon not to hear about the progress of his nemesis, Scott Beaumont, moving up to the top echelons of the public service. Catching the eye of the Prime Minister for his work on the Porter task force, Beaumont, assigned leading a major study on the potential for a massive resource development program in Canada's North, much favored by the PM. David Preston, Porter's Cabinet Secretary, was very upset by Porter's choice off Beaumont over the one he had recommended. Concerned by the rapid rise of this young upstart, decided to take steps to slow it down. Phil Donner learning this from a contact close to Porter quickly passed this choice item on to Muldoon, suggesting he follow it up. Tony did helped by an unexpected source, Barry Green, a John Braxton staff member.

Green sought out Muldoon at the Press Club, finding him enjoying his Friday night double scotch ritual, this one unrestricted, Anne home in Toronto looking after her mother convalescing from a lung infection. Sitting in the lounge nursing his drink saw Green standing at the bar, surveying the room as if looking for someone, spotting Muldoon waved, ordered two drinks.

Moving across the room to join him, "Well Tony, thought I'd find you here, how's the newspaper business?" he asked, handing Tony a double scotch.

"Fine, not bad at all, and you?" Muldoon guardedly replied.

"Can't complain, your column seems to be going well. Although some of your stuff is pure bullshit, you do come up with an occasional gem." he grudgingly admitted.

"Well, I don't make the contents of my articles up. I report what I've been told after checking it out David!" Muldoon replied, controlling his temper.

Green, looking at his watch, replied, "I have to leave shortly. Look Tony, I meant no offense, what i really wanted to tell you is that your old buddy Scott Beaumont has had a falling out with David Preston and doesn't know it yet!"

"What do you mean?" Tony asked, wanting to hear more.

Lowering his voice, quickly looking around not wanting to be overheard, told Muldoon a mutual friend of his and Preston informed him the Cabinet Secretary was as mad as hell at the PM's rejection of his recommended candidate to the lead crucial Northern resources study, selecting Beaumont instead, had a heated discussion with the PM over the issue. Preston offered to resign. Porter refused it assuring Preston he wouldn't overrule him on such matters in the future.

Finishing, on leaving Green remarked, "Well Tony, I don't think Scott is going any further as long as Preston is around."

Muldoon replying, "Thanks David, I owe you a big one."

Noting what he learned from Green strongly confirmed the information on the matter given to him by Donner decided to shelve the current article he was writing, replacing it with one on the Preston - Beaumont conflict, completing it over the weekend in time for inclusion in the Tribune's Monday edition. Muldoon dearly wishing he could witness Beaumont's reaction reading his column, learned his reaction in a way he didn't expect.

Muldoon unexpectedly received an invitation, his first, to one of Nick Gregorian's private parties whose invitees usually included the great or nearly great government members as well as a few press pundits. Batching it alone at home, Anne still in Toronto caring for her mother, Muldoon was looking forward to a night at the Oasis, closed to the public for the event. Arriving at the club shortly after nine pm the night of the event, felt a certain satisfaction being recognized at the door, not having to produce his invitation. Escorted to the bar by a very attractive short-skirted waitress, surprised to see a large glass of scotch waiting for him, as well as the crowded room of specially invited guests.

Leaning against the bar busy identifying some of the more interesting people present felt his elbow being tugged turned quickly seeing a beautifully dressed smiling Cathy Wilson. Kissing him on the cheek, took his hand leading him over to meet Gregorian standing with a small circle of his guests which included a tall beautifully dressed, gorgeous long blonde haired woman. Tony froze in his tracks, it was Carole Beaumont! Shocked let go of Cathy's hand, deciding to leave. Turning around, bumped into an angry looking Scott Beaumont accompanied by Paula and Craig Johnson.

Muldoon, about to walk away was roughly pulled aside by Beaumont, "I want a word with you Muldoon!"

"We don't have anything to talk about Beaumont!" Tony retorted turning to leave, his temper rising.

"Oh yes we do! That garbage you wrote about Preston and me was scandalous. I could sue you and your damn paper for defamation of character".

Regaining his composure, exuding confidence, Tony replied, "I don't think so! It was carefully checked out by our lawyers before it was printed."

"Don't be so damn sure Muldoon." Beaumont fumed.

Muldoon recognizing he was bluffing, Beaumont would be a fool drawing more attention to the matter. Now fully confident in himself, pushed Beaumont aside telling him if he ever wanted to settle this in the alley he would be available, at any time. Beaumont replied asking if that was the only way Tony resolved problems, Muldoon replied smugly, he didn't, instead wrote a column read by thousands.

CHAPTER 20
The Montreal Symposium

A few days after being confronted by Beaumont at the Oasis, Thornton asked Muldoon to cover a symposium for public sector information officers in Montreal later in the week, an assignment he appreciated. It would give him a break from the Ottawa routine, as well as putting him in a better frame of mind before his wife's return from Toronto the following weekend. The symposium hotel being adjacent to the railway station, Tony decided to take the early morning train.

Arriving at the station shortly before his train's departure, heading to the magazine stand to buy a Tribune, on arriving, surprised to see Paula Johnson thumbing through a magazine, hesitated speaking to her, embarrassed over his hasty departure from the Oasis.

Seeing him, she greeted him, smiling, "Hello Tony, what brings you here at this early hour, sniffing out some public service scandal?" she asked, laughing.

"No, are you aware of any I should know?" he responded

playfully, continuing, "As a matter of fact I'm covering a symposium on what you public service information gathering types are up to, and you?"

"You're going to the Info Can symposium? So am I, as a member a panel discussing information policy and its impact on government operations."

"Sounds very impressive and so bureaucratic!" he replied grinning, adding, "Are you travelling alone?"

"Yes, as a matter of fact I am."

"Well then, why don't we sit together?"

"I'd like that Tony." she replied eagerly. They were interrupted by an announcement their train was boarding. Carrying his small overnight case in one hand, her suitcase in the other, following his attractive companion to the boarding exit.

Settling comfortably in their seats, Paula raised the incident at the Oasis, "You certainly left in a hurry the other night. Scott Beaumont was livid over your article about him and Preston, was that the reason?" she asked looking at him intently.

Hesitating before replying, "Yes, partly, he didn't like reading the truth."

Paula having heard rumors substantiating the article's content, dropped the subject, opening a magazine, he a newspaper, each preoccupied with their own thoughts. Paula seemed unaware of the admiring glances of the two men seated across the aisle. Tony, pleased to be in the company of a woman as strikingly beautiful as Paula Johnson.

Muldoon, brooding over the memory of Oasis incident murmured to himself, "The hell with Scott Beaumont, I'm not going to let that bastard ruin this trip!" he muttered turning his attention to his companion.

"Did you say something Tony?" she asked,

"No Paula,, just thinking out loud."

After checking into the hotel, Tony's, asked Paula to have lunch with him later. She declined, having a lunch commitment with the other panel members, agreeing to meet with him for cocktails and dinner after the afternoon session. Muldoon arriving at the cocktail lounge shortly after five pm looked around to see if Paula had arrived not seeing her, selected a table near the entrance to the lounge. Twenty minutes, two double scotches later, she arrived, breathless, apologizing for the delay, rising, warmly shaking her hand, seated Paula beside him.

"Sorry to be so late, there were so many after session questions. How was your session?"

"Fine, quite interesting. What would you like to drink Paula?"

"A vodka, martini, very dry, thanks Tony."

They spent the next hour comparing notes on their sessions, snidely laughing at the antics of people at other tables showing the effect of too many fast drinks, avoided mentioning their marriage partners. About to order yet another round, stopped by Paula saying they should have something to eat first, Tony agreed, asking her where she would like to go, Montreal boasting of some of the finest restaurants in the country, she replying, since the hotel had a fine dining room why not dine there. Tony heartily agreeing offered to pick her up at her room, she demurred suggesting they meet at the dining room entrance.

When Paula arrived looking fabulous in a form-fitting black dress, doing full justice to her superb figure and lovely legs. Tony caught his breath at the stunning sight of his beautiful dinner companion, regretted he hadn't brought his good suit. Smiling, she taking both of his hands, after he enthusiastically complimented her on her appearance, apologizing for his.

"You look fine Tony, let's go in, I'm famished."

During a delightful dinner, outside of a few perfunctory remarks, didn't make reference to Paula's husband, Craig or Tony's wife, Anne, speaking mainly about themselves. Finishing an after dinner coffee

Paula taking her dinner partner's hand said stifling a yawn, "Tony, I've really enjoyed this. It's been a long day, I think I'll turn in."

Muldoon alarmed," So soon? At least, let's have a night cap."

"Oh very well, only one mind you."

One became two and then three, having a great time speculating about the other couples sitting around them, surprised by the number of young women with considerably older men.

"I have it Paula, the hotel is hosting father- daughter convention."

"I don't think so Tony, it looks more like a grandfather-granddaughter one to me," both laughing, overheard by a nearby couple glowering angrily at them. Paula, reaching over the table touched Muldoon's arm, "Tony, it's time to go."

Looking at the angry couple, he agreeing, she picking up her purse, they left the dining room, heading towards the bank of elevators.

Waiting for the elevator. Paula laughingly commented, "Maybe not a father - daughter convention but a reunion of dirty old men!"

Arriving at her door Paula fumbled in her purse for her door key.

Tony, took the purse from her hands, saying, "Here let me help you", quickly finding her key, opened her door. Following her into the room. she stopped, turned around, touching his cheek, saying, softly, "Tony it's late, you really should be going." Not replying, took her in his arms kissing her passionately. At first her body tightened like a knot, then relaxed.

Weakly trying pushing him away she murmured, "No Tony. No!" trying to break from his embrace, stopped, threw her arms around his neck, digging her fingers into his back, their tongues met. Quickly undressing each other, he carefully removing her black dress, underwear and stockings, pulled back the covers of her bed. For the next hour, they lost all sense of time until falling into a deep sleep, her head nestled on his shoulder.

Later, although his shoulder was aching from the weight of Paula's head, hesitated moving it not wanting to wake her, was startled by her voice, "Are you awake Tony?"

"Yes I am." Muldoon replied, relieved now able to move her head.

"We were terribly wrong doing this you know!" she replied, her voice anxious, guilt ridden.

Sitting up, Tony turned on the bed lamp at his side, she joining him taking a package of cigarettes out of her purse handing it and a lighter to Muldoon who lit up two giving one to Paula, leaning back against her pillow began talking about her marriage, "It was terrific at first, two good careers, enough money to do the things you wanted."

"What does that all mean?" he asked.

Thinking for a moment she replied, "It means you can have two of everything. " blowing a cloud of smoke into the air.

"Is that all? Who are you going to give all these things and money to, after you're gone?"

"Who cares what happens after you're dead!" Paula responded, blowing another cloud of smoke into the air. Taking the cigarette out of her hand, butted it in the ashtray beside him, leaned over taking her in his arms.

"Oh Tony, not again!" Paula protested.

"Oh yes, Again! And again! " he responded, his voice hoarse with passion.

At a late breakfast, she started to talk about Scott after assured by Muldoon, nothing she said would appear in print, confirmed Beaumont was having serious difficulties with Preston who was looking for a way to get rid of him, believing Beaumont's big problem was wanting Preston's job, taking steps ensuring he would never get it, her husband thinking the same. As they left the restaurant, stopping at the door, looking intently at each other, she gently touched his face, saying softly, "Tony dear, it was wonderful but never again, there's too much at stake! Goodbye."

Leaving, she walking down the street in one direction, he walking up the other.

CHAPTER 21

The Bribery Scandal Scoop

Arriving home, entering the apartment shocked seeing Anne sitting in the living room, having returned early from her lengthy Toronto visit, aware from a regular evening phone call he'd be attending a Montreal conference. Regaining his composure, Tony dropped his small bag, going over to her, standing up for his welcoming kiss. Later, over coffee, Anne asked him if anything interesting happened during the session, if he'd met anyone he knew. Hesitating momentarily, mentioned Paula Johnson.

She said laughing, " Dressed to the teeth, I'll bet."

Picking up a newspaper, Tony replied, "I didn't really notice."

The week following his Montreal visit, Paula Johnson, relieved Muldoon had kept his word, sent him an unsigned note saying simply 'Thanks for everything!'

Included in the bundle of mail containing Paula Johnsons' note, were three plain brown envelopes, leaning back in his chair, yawning, saying, "What were some disgruntled servants complaining about now?"

The first two he opened, contained the usual litany of complaints of prejudice, unfairness, promotion denials, which he threw into a large basket beside his desk, filled with similar complaints, the third was different, making him sit up. This unsigned letter containing one carefully typed page, purporting John Braxton, being in serious financial trouble, accepted a large bribe to pay off his debts, finishing by saying more information would be coming substantiating this claim. Quickly leaving his desk, went to see his editor, Jack Thornton.

Reading the letter, Thornton, stroking his jaw thoughtfully, "Could it be just another crank letter?"

"No, I don't think so, it's logical, too well written, I have a gut feeling whoever wrote this knows what he's talking about!" Muldoon replied.

"Well, this is political dynamite Tony, start digging around, meanwhile, I'll speak to Mister Marsden. I know he'll want to hear about this." he exclaimed.

About to tell Thornton he'd been made aware of Braxton's financial problems before joining the Tribune, Tony held back, feeling it would be betraying a confidence and Braxton had been fair and helpful when he needed it. It turned out, the publisher was keenly interested in the Braxton matter, requesting Thornton assign Phil Donner to assist Muldoon in following it up.

Shortly after, Muldoon received a second letter, also unsigned, written in the same neat style containing data alleging to confirm John Braxton had received fifty thousand dollars, from a Nick Gregorian, a front man for a Montreal based crime Syndicate. Braxton was to use his influence to help a notorious international drug dealer, identified as a Boris Aristine, a man known to the

RCMP and the Immigration department, enter Canada legally as a landed immigrant. This allegation confirmation by Donner learning from a reliable Liberal source during a three martini lunch, Braxton had recently paid off his debts. Even without this, the recently re-elected Liberal minority government was under relentless attack in the House of Commons over alleged impropriety regarding several large land transactions in Ontario and Quebec reported by Muldoon in recent columns. Marsden authorized the introduction of the Gregorian matter in a deliberately vague way avoiding possible litigation, in a upcoming Muldoon patronage article to test reader reaction and with Donner's help, delve further into this politically explosive issue.

Their information checked out, learning from an RCMP narcotics investigation contact. Boris Aristine was a prime suspect as the leader of a major drug smuggling international ring, operating in Europe and the Middle East using as a front a prosperous, legitimate cosmetics import - export business. The whole operation had become the subject of a major investigation by the French police and Interpol, aware Aristine was looking for a legitimate way leaving Europe, setting up the center of his operation in Canada. On learning this, after consulting his legal advisors, Marsden gave Thornton the green light for - Muldoon and Donner, in a joint by-line, splashing the sordid story over the Tribune's front page, creating a storm of angry reaction across the country. Its political impact was catastrophic for the scandal plagued liberal minority government.

Initially, a series of angry denials by the involved Ministers, followed by hollow threats of legal action had no effect changing the public's initial reaction to the shoddy business. A weak admission by the Prime Minister of an unfortunate mistake, the resignations of the Ministers named, failed to quell the furor in the House over yet another government generated scandal. Reluctantly, the Conservatives supported a New Democratic Party sponsored Vote of Non-Confidence motion, easily carried in the House, a number of Liberals abstaining.

Thornton, Muldoon and Donner were elated, with a jubilant Marsden, proposed a toast in his office, to their unknown benefactor, the author of the damning unsigned letters. Later relocating to Thornton's house, the three got royally drunk. For once, Anne didn't mind, it was a great day for her husband.

The following morning, discussing the previous day's events with Donner, Muldoon expressed surprise at the Publisher's high spirited reaction learned the reason, the main government actor in this political drama, Big John Braxton, who some years earlier, broke up his marriage taking his wife away from him. On the night of the election, watching it in the Publisher's office, the defeat of the Liberals certain, the Conservatives likely to form a minority government. The resurging New Democratic Party, under its new, energetic young leader, Jake Enright, once again holding the balance of power.

Marsden exclaimed, "This will teach those bastards a lesson, especially Donald Porter. As for that son of a bitch, Braxton, when they jail him, I hope they throw away the key!"

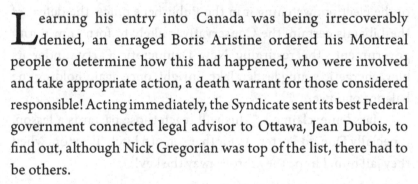

CHAPTER 22

Scandal Revelation Impact

Learning his entry into Canada was being irrecoverably denied, an enraged Boris Aristine ordered his Montreal people to determine how this had happened, who were involved and take appropriate action, a death warrant for those considered responsible! Acting immediately, the Syndicate sent its best Federal government connected legal advisor to Ottawa, Jean Dubois, to find out, although Nick Gregorian was top of the list, there had to be others.

Muldoon and Donner benefited significantly from their Gregorian scandal expose, receiving generous bonuses and healthy salary increases, Muldoon's Dancing around the Hill column was syndicated. He was accredited to the Press Gallery, regularly interviewed by the television media, resulting in an envious colleague remarking,

"Tony Baby, you've got it made!"

Despite only achieving a minority government, the Conservatives, under a young, aggressive Grant Talbot took charge, determined to rule as if he had a majority, taking full advantage of the disarray of among the Liberals. He introduced major legislation dealing with the scandals, feeling assured of the support of the New Democratic Party, the party fully aware of the Canadian Public's disgust over the scandal issue, as well as the broad support of the press, especially the Ottawa Tribune.

Muldoon's wife was in seventh heaven, their new financial affluence enabling her to afford things she had only dreamt about. It started with a holiday trip to Mexico then moving into an upscale apartment building bordering the Rideau canal, furnishing it in the manner she was accustomed to before her marriage. There was one notable exception, Tony insisted on keeping his father's old oak desk and beat up leather recliner. Late one night, leaning back in the recliner nursing a large scotch, wondered how all this was impacting on Scott Beaumont.

Scott Beaumont, receiving an unexpected phone call from Cathy Wilson was unsettled by the pained urgency in her voice, set up a luncheon meeting at a nearby restaurant to discuss what she described to be 'a very serious personal matter' affecting both of them. Beaumont entering their meeting place, seeing her sitting at a secluded corner both table, toying with an empty martini glass her eyes brimming with tears, taking a deep breath, joined her.

Cathy greeted him, saying, "I hope you'll forgive the dramatics Scott, I had to see you!"

"Yes Cathy, what is this all about?" looking around ensuring they couldn't be overheard.

"You know I've been seeing a lot of Nick Gregorian, actually more than just seeing him, well, lately he's seeing someone else!"

"What's that got to do with me Cathy?"

"It's you wife!"

"You can't be serious making a shocking allegation like that, you must be crazy!" retorting in anger.

"Crazy am I? Well, I watched them last Thursday night, saw her leaving his apartment at one in the morning. I suspected he was seeing another woman on the sly the past few months never imagining it could be her!"she retorted in a hate-filled voice.

Momentarily stunned, recalling Carole's Thursday night sessions with the 'girls', a shocked Beaumont replied quietly, "You're sure about this, Cathy??"

"Dead sure, I'm sorry Scott." Beaumont, standing up to leave was stopped by Cathy saying, "Wait, there's more."

Over the next hour, she told Beaumont what she knew about the whole business between Braxton and Gregorian, Nick paying off the Minister's debts with Montreal money for his help expediting the entrance into Canada of someone from Paris, the clandestine visitors from Montreal, Gregorian's nervousness after these visits, her refusing to believe Gregorian was only using her to get to Braxton.

When she finished, Scott, shaking his head in disbelief asked, "Cathy, these allegations are very serious. Is there any concrete proof supporting them?"

She replied, " Yes, there is Scott! His diary and specially numbered bank account as well as a tape Nicky made of the transaction with John."

Scott asked, " Do you think you could make a copy of the tape and all the rest?"

She answered "Yes, I'm sure I can."

He left, promising her she wouldn't be implicated in any way by anything he did with the information, in turn, having her promise keeping her knowledge of his wife's involvement with Gregorian strictly to herself.

That evening after dinner, Carole remarked how quiet he was, picking up the newspaper Scott replied, he had a lot on his mind. Thursday evening, seeing Carole dressed up for her regular evening 'with the girls'.

Beaumont sarcastically commented, "Aren't you a little overdressed for an evening with your friends?"

Startled by Scott's unusual comment on her regular Thursday night outings, replied, "Well, you know the girls, always trying to outdo each other."

Beaumont, about to question her about her 'friends' remained silent.

Reaching the door, turning her head, said, "Don't wait up for me, you know what women are like when they get together, absolutely no sense o time when they start to talk."

"Yes indeed you bitch!" he muttered to himself as she closed the door. Exercising his remarkable self-control, deciding this was not the time to raise his wife's involvement with the Florentine possibly undermining his career and future, would remain quiet, turning his attention to the paper, looking to see if a Muldoon column was featured. As for his wife? It was all over, he deciding how and when.

Shortly before the election, David Preston, in the Prime Minister's office, Porter asking, "David, do we have any idea where this damning leak came from? Not that it really matters now." his voice choking with emotion.

"No Prime Minister, the Royal Canadian Mounted Police are investigating it, so far, haven't any leads."

"What about the Tribune? Couldn't it be obliged to reveal their evidence to the government?"

"No sir, it would only make matters worse according to our best legal advisors, who believe the Tribune, being a strong Tory supporter, would fight us over the issue of source protection."

"Well then, that's it, we'll probably never know. " Porter replied sighing.

Preston added, "According to Inspector Guthrie, leading the investigation, it has to be someone with linkages to both Braxton and Gregorian, he's dead certain about that, he's one o the RCMP's best."

Shortly after breaking the 'Gregorian Affair' in the Tribune, Muldoon was visited by Inspector Guthrie, "Thank you for seeing me on such short notice, Mister Muldoon."

"No problem, Inspector, what can I do for you?" Tony replied guardedly, leading him to a small office reserved for privacy.

After seating himself, Guthrie got right to the point, "The allegations in your column are very serious indicating criminal intent on the part of a senior government member. There are two major issues here, the nature o the information you have and the identity of the sender."

Tony, relaxing a little, smiled replying, "As for the first issue, I think I'll be able to help you if our lawyers agree, as for the second, I don't know who sent it, if I did, I couldn't tell you."

"Come, come Mister Muldoon confidential source privilege is a fiction out of the cinema."

"I wouldn't call it fiction Inspector, in any event it's a matter for our lawyers to deal with."

"Now, now Mister Muldoon, I'm not here to create problems between us, I'm just looking for the truth. Because of its criminal nature, surely you wouldn't object to my seeing the material your more serious allegations are based on."

"No, not at all. I've discussed with our management and lawyers who have agreed as long as one of our legal team is present."

"That's fine with me Mister Muldoon, if tomorrow afternoon at one pm is convenient, I'll bring along two of my investigators."

"Sounds alright to me, I'll speak with my editor, if there any problems I'll let you know."

"Good Mister Muldoon, here's my card." then Guthrie left.

The RCMP investigation led to both Braxton and Gregorian charged with bribery under section 99 of the Criminal Code, the results being disastrous for both men, Braxton, not only defeated in the subsequent election, facing a jail term and bankrupt. For Gregorian, it was far worse, the relationship between Gregorian with Boris Aristine and the Montreal Syndicate revealed in the court proceedings. The Syndicate members in Paris and Montreal were enraged, not only many months of effort wasted, also the huge financial investment lost in the now closed Oasis.

Nick Gregorian was frightened, having unsuccessfully tried to contact the Montreal Syndicate, worried his phone was being tapped by the RCMP, wouldn't answer, had to mortgage everything he owned to raise his bail, ended his relationship with a distraught Carole Beaumont, concluding her husband may have had something to do with the leak to the press, somehow having been made aware of her affair. Gregorian wanted to run, didn't know how or where.

CHAPTER 23

Syndicate Retribution

Gregorian's fate was decided at a late night Syndicate Montreal meeting involving major drug dealers from Canada and the United States, the last item on their agenda involved little discussion, concluding Gregorian had been too involved with women, that an example had to be made of him as a warning to other members. The hit man selected, one o the best albeit the most expensive, had only one price, fifty thousand dollars with half up front and the rest when the job was done, his name, Jorge Manoff, a boyhood friend of Aristine, his specialty, the garrote.

Jorge Manoff, a product of the short, stocky powerfully built hill people of Macedonia while just a boy, during his peoples' war against the Italians, then the Germans, learned the art of killing from his father, leader of an insurgent band sequestered in the hills. Only ten years old killed his first man at the urging of his father, a young German soldier almost a boy himself, tightly bound on a chair, his fear-filled face silently pleading for mercy. Jorge's father called his son over handing him his German luger automatic asked him to cock it as he had trained him to do, said, "Kill him!' Jorge, dismayed, hesitated, holding the gun limply in his hands.

His father slapping his son's face hard, angrily repeated his order, "Obey! Kill him! Now!'

Holding his father's luger in both hands, cocked it, pointing it at the terrified young German captive's head, shot him.

"Good boy! Now we eat." Jorge's father responded, patting him fondly on the head.

After the war, Jorge evolved into a professional killer, completely dispassionate about it, his trade, a high paying enterprise, becoming a master at avoiding detection, gaining entrance into his victim's homes. His preferred killing method, the garrote, hating guns since shooting the young German years earlier. The technique for using this unusual weapon, taught him by one of his father's band members, the weapon itself, easy to construct, conceal, readily disposable. The construction of the weapon, simple and quick, required a loop of thinly stranded wire and two detachable wooden handles. His killing technique very effective, quickly moving behind his victims, looping the wire around their necks, with crossed hands pulling the handles apart with a powerful snapping motion resulting in the victim's instant death. Manoff became so expert at this technique, he seldom broke his victim's skin.

Nick Gregorian finally heard from his Montreal Syndicate contact, reassuring him, although some of the members were upset, he was considered too valuable to the organization to be punished for his mistakes, had nothing to worry about, would be contacted the following day by one of their best government contact lawyers, Jean Dubois. The meeting took place on a park bench beside the Rideau canal. Dubois all sympathy and understanding, endeavored to reassure a very nervous, agitated Gregorian,

"Nick my boy, not to worry, we're going to take care of everything.

I'm arranging with one of the top government connected law firms to represent you, pinning this whole mess on that bastard Braxton. You'll get off lightly, probably nothing at all, the organization has big plans for you."

"Jean, be honest be honest with me. Am I being set up?"

"What? You being set up? Don't be ridiculous Nick. They never would have sent me here to see you if that was the case, not at my price! Look, I'll show you." He produced the business cards of two prominent Ottawa lawyers, "These are the people who are going to represent you with my help, satisfied?"

Gregorian, feeling reassured, gratefully took the cards. After talking for another ten minutes, Dubois, looking at his watch stood up, "Nick, I must go. I have to be back in Montreal tonight. Call one of those names tomorrow for the details."

After shaking hands, Dubois left quickly. Greatly relieved, Gregorian left for his apartment. In the elevator, riding to his floor, began humming a popular Italian song, not feeling this relaxed for days. Opening his door entered, taking off his jacket threw it on a chair still humming, deciding to call Cathy Wilson, went over to his phone table not seeing Jorge Manoff standing in the shadows of the kitchen, about to pick up his phone felt a sharp snap around his neck, nothing more.

The following morning, his cleaning woman arriving for her regular tidying up of the apartment, on opening the door, let out a wall-shaking scream.

Inspector Ronald Guthrie, accompanied by an Ottawa police detective sergeant arrived to inspect the body guarded by a young, ashen faced police officer. "Damndest thing I've ever seen, Sergeant!" he said, sweating profusely, sick to his stomach.

The detective sergeant didn't reply instead turned to Guthrie, "Let's have a look." Raising the top of the sheet covering the face of the corpse, both men gasping in amazement, seeing Gregorian flat on his back, his penis stuck in his mouth!

The grim-faced constable exclaimed," What kind of pervert would do a thing like that?"

Ignoring the question, Guthrie looking at the red wet around the body's neck, spoke, "That's real professional job Hal, he didn't break the skin. Look at the poor bastard's eyes, he didn't know what hit him."

The police sergeant replying, "What about the dick in the mouth business Ron, how do you explain that?"

Guthrie replied, "The dick? I'm almost certain this was a Syndicate authorized hit, a warning to the others to lay off the women, he was a real Don Juan, we'd been watching him for awhile trying to get a line on his Montreal Syndicate connection, you wouldn't believe the identity of some of the women he was sleeping with."

Looking down on the shocking state of Gregorian's corpse, Guthrie's police companion ruefully commented, "Well, he sure as hell is finished sleeping with women now!"

The coroner, held up by traffic, finally arriving, started examining the body. More police arrived to check around the building to see if anyone had heard or seen anything, Guthrie, dubious they would. Turning to Guthrie the detective sergeant exclaimed,

"Let's get the hell out of here, I need a drink!"

"Ok after I make a phone call." Guthrie called Tony Muldoon.

Muldoon, shaken by Guthrie's call, feeling partly responsible for Gregorian's ghastly death, was very upset, called Jack Thornton with the news, who was ecstatic, "What a scoop! We'll get on it right away. Look, Tony, that tail hound's death isn't your fault, you were only doing your job as a good newspaper man. I'll have Phil write this up. Why don't you go to the club for a stiff drink?"

A downcast Muldoon, not objecting, after briefing Donner, left for the Press Club, after quickly downing a double scotch, making sure he couldn't be overheard, phoned his wife, "Anne, Nick Gregorian is dead." his voice quivering.

Shocked she replied, " Dead? How? In an accident?"

"No, he was murdered, I'll tell you more about it later." Tony replied.

"Where are you Tony?"

"At the Club."

"You come home this instant. It won't do any good trying to drown your sorrows with scotch, his death wasn't your fault." she said reassuringly.

Learning of Gregorian's death in brief radio report, Carole Beaumont was shattered, having grown to love him in a way she had never loved her husband, her Florentine lover having awakened in her emotions and desires she didn't know existed, now he was dead. Beginning to cry stopped, she had to be careful Scott didn't see her this way, she'd make up an excuse to visit her mother, with the 'indifferent way he had treated her lately felt certain he wouldn't mind.

When Scott came home late that evening. the newspaper under his arm, handed to her saying bitingly, "Looks like a good friend of yours has come to a bad end."

"Whatever do you mean " she demanded tears welling in her eyes.

"You know damn well what I mean, Carole, your bloody Italian lover has been murdered, and you know what? He was found with his penis stuck in his mouth!" Beaumont added triumphantly.

His wife, her breath coming in short gasps, not able to respond, quickly left shutting herself up in their bedroom, staying there until her husband left the following morning.

Gregorian's death, a hollow victory for Cathy Wilson, still loving him despite being used, heart sick having helped destroy the two men she was closest to. Aided by Scott Beaumont, arranging a job for her in Industry department's communications division. Despite being heartbroken, she quickly adapted, she had to survive. Meanwhile Beaumont was busy, skillfully making known his political preference for the Conservatives, ensuring the new Prime Minister's office and Privy Council office were aware of this.

CHAPTER 24

Scott Beaumont - Deputy Minister

The new PCO, anxious to replace a number of Deputy Ministers, whose careers had been nurtured under years of Liberal' government leadership, with younger, politically reliable new blood, drew up a list of potential candidates with Scott Beaumont's name near its top. Within a month of the Conservatives forming a government, Beaumont was appointed the Deputy Minister of Regional Development, George Arnott's last job before retiring, by the new Clerk of the Privy Council, a man highly regarded and trusted by the Prime Minister but reputed having serious health problems.

The newly appointed Minister of Beaumont's department was Rowena Butler, a young, attractive, hard driving, self-made, take no prisoners, successful loyal Conservative politician from British Columbia whose tenacity and vote getting strength, earned her a Cabinet position in Grant Talbot's government. Beaumont wondering how he would relate o this political dynamo, impatiently awaited her call. He didn't have a long wait.

Beaumont's feelings were mixed approaching John Braxton's old office for their first meeting with his new Minister, having researched her background, reading some of her political speeches. He learned from a Western Conservative she was living in an open marriage with a successful Vancouver business man, valuing friendly compatibility over a sexual relationship, made aware she had been involved in a short close relationship with her long serving political adviser, now her Chief of Staff, Peter Savage, terminating when her political fortunes were on the rise. It was Savage who met Beaumont in the Ministers outer office, taking an instant dislike to Butler's, tall, handsome, well dressed, new Deputy.

Extending a hand in a tentative gesture of friendship, "I'm Peter Savage Rowena's, no, I mean the Minister's Chief of Staff."

"Yes, I've heard of you." Beaumont responded coldly, grasping Savage's extended hand in a firm grip.

"Let's go in, the Minister's waiting." Beaumont followed the short, sandy colored hair, sallow faced -Savage into the Minister's office, finding it strange returning to the office he had associated with John Braxton. Rowena Butler, rising from her desk, beckoned them to the small sitting room adjacent to her office. Shaking hands with Beaumont, impressed by the firmness of her grip, pleasantly surprised by this mature, very attractive woman.

Rowena Butler was a striking looking woman, a natural brunette, tall, full figured, attractive legs, smartly dressed in a plaid skirt and tartan jacket and a white blouse, partly unbuttoned accentuating the curvature of her firm bosom. She in turn, intrigued by the appearance, dress and handsomeness of her tall Deputy whose deeply set blue eyes matched hers, her reaction to meeting Beaumont quickly noticed by the perceptive Savage.

The Minister commenced, "Well it looks like we're both new on the job although I saw from your personnel file you previously served in the department."

"Yes Minister, after heading a task force, I was appointed Assistant Deputy Minister for Regional Development."

"That's great, that's an area my government wants to concentrate on, especially as it applies to the Western provinces' small business development which I imagine isn't news to you?"

"No, not really Minister, although the focus of my work in the past, was mainly on Ontario and Quebec."

"You mean where the Liberal voting strength was." Butler replied, smiling.

Not answering, Beaumont smiled back.

"Probably the Windsor area." Savage interjected, frowning. upset at witnessing a warm chemistry developing between Rowena and Scott.

Butler suddenly turned to Savage, "Peter, would you get the notes I made after I met with the PM yesterday?"

When Savage left, Rowena turned to Scott, "You'll have to excuse Peter, the Chief of Staff thing is new to him, he's loyally worked for me for years, very politically well connected in my riding. As soon as he returns I'll give you the essence of my meeting with the Prime Minister, when you've had a chance to think about it, we'll talk."

"Minister, would you like to set up a regular meeting schedule?"

"Yes, of course, how would Friday morning at nine suit you? It follows my Thursday meetings with the PM giving me an opportunity updating on anything relevant to the department."

"Fine Minister, Friday mornings a nine it is."

Savage returned with her notes, reading them she looked up at Scott, "The PM intends to increase the level of support for small business i the West by fifty percent over the next four years and wants to review our plans for doing his as soon as possible preferably by the end of the month, Can you do it?"

"Yes, of course. Minister." As they stood up, Scott preparing to leave.

Shaking his hand she warmly replied, "Good. I've a feeling we're going to get along just fine, don't you think so Peter?" smiling, turning to her aid,

"Yes, I'm sure we will." Savage replied half heartedly.

It didn't take Beaumont long establishing himself in the department, its senior officers nervous of the change of government, eager to please, were relieved to have a Deputy who knew the department and them, with his Minister who frequently phoned him asking him to her office, sometimes phoning him at home. The calls tolerated by his wife back in Ottawa after a long stay at her Toronto Rosedale home, urged by her mother, accepted a marriage of convenience for the sake of Scott's career.

CHAPTER 25

Scott Beaumont and Rowena Butler - Lovers

As the weeks passed, Beaumont, preoccupied with the task given by Butler, after their frequent late hour meetings, she often asked him to join her for a drink produced from Braxton's small bar, the only piece of furniture of his remaining in the office. Peter Savage, increasingly resentful of Beaumont's presence, often tried to join them like a watchful hound. After weeks of hard work, numerous revisions, Scott finishing the report requested by Butler for submission to the Prime Minister, briefed her on its essential points at a regular Friday morning meeting, leaving a copy for her to read.

About to leave was stopped by Rowena asking, "Look Scott, I'm going to read this cover to cover over the weekend at a cottage I've rented in the Gatineau, when could I get hold of you if I have any questions?"

Looking surprised, Beaumont replied, "Minister I'll be at home most of the weekend, feel free to call me at any time."

Rowena, paused for a moment catching her breath asked him, "On second thought, as this is very important to the PM, it would be better if you would drive up to my place tomorrow afternoon. I know I'll have a lot of questions to be ready for when I meet him next week leaving us little time to discuss it at work, do you think you could manage it ?"

"Of course Minister, how do I get there?" Smiling, Rowena gave Scott the route to her cottage." That sounds easy, at what time"

She eagerly replied, "Say around four, we can have a drink and supper afterwards."

The following day, Beaumont had little trouble finding Butler's charming rustic cottage located by a small clear water lake. Parking his car beside hers, strode to the front, finding Rowena, having heard his car coming, standing in the doorway of her cedar log cabin, smiling broadly, ushered him into its living room. Taking his brief case out of his hand placed it on a chair next to a large fireplace.

"I'll pour you a drink then we'll sit out front, the view of the lake and the sunset is gorgeous." She was dressed in figure clinging slacks, a bulky Norwegian style sweater similar to the one worn by Beaumont, a flowery brown scarf around her neck, a very attractive looking pair. After seating himself beside Rowena, Scott enquired about her reaction reading the report,

"Oh yes, the report, let's discuss it after supper. By the way Scott, away from the office please call me Rowena. Now you tell me, what should come first the report, or our drink?" she demanded, laughing.

"Both I guess, Rowena." he replied smiling broadly.

"A very political answer I'd better get our supper started. I'll call you when its ready."

Rowena expertly prepared two large steaks smothered in onions, a tangy salad, produced a bottle of vintage red wine. The early night becoming cool, she asked Scott to prepare a fire which he did, careful to prevent ashes from spilling on deep pile large wool rug fronting the stone fireplace. After eating, Rowena, producing two snifter glasses of cognac handed one to Scott, seating herself on the rug in front of the fireplace, motioned Beaumont to join her. They chatted as the sun set over the Gatineau hills, she telling him of her British Columbia childhood on her father's large prosperous apple farm, her early involvement in Conservative politics.

She still not referring to the report, Beaumont broached the subject, "By the way Rowena, what do you think of the report?"

Looking surprised she responded, "The report, yes the report, let's toast it." raising her glass clinking his glass.

He now sitting close to her. "Shouldn't we discuss it now?"

"It's not necessary Scott, I read it last night, it's fine just the way it is."

"Then what?"

Putting a finger against his lips, she murmured, "Don't be naive Scott, I want you to make love to me!"

"I know." he replied taking her in his arms. They lay stretched out on the rug, making love into the small hours of the morning in front of the crackling fire, he not caring how his wife would react to his all night absence.

Scott Beaumont's common sense told him becoming romantically involved with Rowena Butler was a high risk situation, one that could end his promising career in the Public Service. He didn't care finding her the perfect match for his relentless drive and ambition, qualities she shared with him, including her skilled perception of complex economic and political issues, ability effectively dealing with her equally ambitious colleagues, all of which recognized by a Prime Minister having big plans for this female prodigy from the West,

Beaumont sagely concluding, "If you're going to hitch your wagon to a star, then this was one well worth the risk."

They met frequently, restricting their love-making interludes to her Gatineau cottage, becoming a second home for Beaumont, an arrangement hated by his wife and Peter Savage, both in no position to do anything about it.

Their relationship was more than a love match, Beaumont, successfully produced a series of papers dealing with the regional disparity in Canada of unemployment levels, greatly impressing the Prime Minister, resulting in Butler being made a member of his inner Cabinet, Talbot choosing to ignore persistent rumors of her personal relationship with her talented Deputy, rumors that the Tribune's publisher refused reported in the paper much to Tony Muldoon's dismay. As Rowena Butler's star rose so did Beaumont's in a few months, becoming the most influential member of the large number of new Deputy Ministers appointed by the Tory government.

It didn't take Carole Beaumont long to realize what was happening, at first guilt- struck over her torrid affair with Gregorian, kept silent, until on his returning from a weekend with Rowena decided to have it out with him. Having just laid down his weekend bag, she placed herself in front of her husband, her eyes blazing, "Did you have a good time with your political whore, Scott? Has she no shame carrying on with an employee, she a married woman and you a married man?"

Scott's face reddened, "I don't know what you're talking about, Carole, let me by." she didn't budge,

"You know very well what I'm talking about, Scott, you're sleeping with your Minister! It's a damn disgrace, you with your high and mighty airs. I can't ever imagining George Arnott ever doing that to keep his job, you a Deputy Minister indeed!"

Angry beyond words, Beaumont picked up his bag, looked pensively at his wife for a moment before replying, "I'm leaving you Carole, I'll phone when I'm settled, then I'll come for the rest of my things."

"So that's it! You've been planning this all along, just like you do everything else. You can leave but it will cost you plenty!"

Now calm, Beaumont replied," I don't think so. Let's not forget your lately departed Nicky and how he died."

"You miserable bastard!" she shouted as he left closing the door.

Driving to a hotel near his office, registered, tempted to phone Rowena, thought better of it, taking a shower went to bed.

Peter Savage, the other party profoundly affected by his Minister's personal relationship with Scott Beaumont, having loved her for years, with the forlorn hope her affair with Beaumont would eventually end, remained quiet for the moment, keeping his intense jealous dislike of Beaumont to himself. Rowena liked Savage, depending on his loyalty, usually sound political advice, knowing he was in love with her, greatly regretted their brief love affair carried out in the heat of a previous election battle. Savage forlornly hoped their ill advised short physical intimacy would someday turn to love.

CHAPTER 26

Muldoon Learns 'He's Been Had' by Beaumont

Grant Talbot, now the Prime Minister of Canada his political destiny, was concerned, resenting the unwanted dependency on the New Democratic Party's support for his minority government, having to compromise with its newly elected leader, Jake Enright, as young and vigorous as himself. He also faced with the increasing disenchantment of the Canadian public over the entire political process, its leadership, numerous scandals, the increasing tensions in the Middle East, the shaky economy. He harbored doubts regarding some of his Cabinet and senior public service appointments, the deteriorating health of his right hand man, Jonathan Rogers, the Secretary of the Cabinet and Clerk of the Privy Council who would soon need to be replaced but by whom?

One name brought to his attention, albeit in a negative way, was Scott Beaumont. Talbot alerted to his rumored affair with one of his treasured Ministers, Rowena Butler, supportive of her very accomplished Deputy, who had also impressed him with his imaginative proposals on regional job development. Talbot concluded, appointing Beaumont to replace Rogers would solve two of his problems, separating Beaumont from Butler helping dispel gossip about their relationship, provide a young competent replacement for his Cabinet Secretary. Having decided, phoned Rogers, Butler and Beaumont in turn. Their reactions predictable, Rogers surprised but supportive, being appointed Ambassador to Washington a much less demanding responsibility, Butler, sorry losing Scott pleased with his appointment, her aid Savage glad to see his nemesis out of the way, Beaumont, ecstatic, always wanting such an appointment, not expecting it so soon.

Tony Muldoon was feeling miserable, no amount of Scotch self flagellation diminishing his regrets over his treatment of his wife when he told her of Beaumont's impending appointment, resulting in Anne, as she had done before, returning to Toronto to be with her mother. For the past month adamantly refused answering any of his calls, despite being urged by her mother to do so. Tony approaching the bar saw Peter Savage heading unsteadily in his direction, turning around retraced his steps hoping to avoid the man he intensely disliked.

He was called by Savage slurring his words, "Hey Muldoon, come over here, I'll buy you a drink;."

"No thanks, some other time." Tony replied heading for the exit.

"Well, OK, have it your own way, I just thought you'd like to hear something really interesting."

Hearing this, a few men sitting nearby perked up their heads, Muldoon stopped in his tracks, the newsman in him taking over, not passing up a news opportunity no matter the source. He led Savage back to his table ordering a Scotch and a refill for Savage.

Sitting down, Tony asked, "What's this all about Peter?"

Waiting for their drinks to arrive, Savage replied looking smug, "Do you know you were had by Scott Beaumont?"

"I've been had by Beaumont? What gave you that crazy idea? That's a lot of garbage Savage and you know it!"

"Garbage? I don't think so. He set you up. He's the one that sent you the dope on Braxton and Gregorian, surely you must have realized that? If you don't want to believe me, why don't you ask Braxton's former assistant Cathy Wilson because that's what she told her room- mate an old girlfriend of mine. What a laugh."

Wanting to punch Savage's smug face, instead stood up, quickly leaving the club thinking, "Could it be possible he was set up? Was Savage just trying to get under his skin?" He had to find out, he'd contact Cathy Wilson. She reluctantly agreed meeting Tony at a small restaurant off the beaten track in Ottawa's Italian district.

After placing their order, Muldoon quickly got to the point, "I've just been told that it was Scott Beaumont that sent me the material on Gregorian and Braxton and you knew all about it. Is it true Cathy?"

Looking frightened, she replied, "What do you mean? Who told you that?"

"Never mind, I'm protecting my source the same way I'll protect you if you help me by telling me the truth. If anyone else gets hold of this before me I won't be able to help you. Well, Cathy?"

Pausing while the waiter poured their wine, sighing, "Tony, you promise you'll keep me out of it?"

"Absolutely!"

"Yes it's true!" she replied choking up.

After calming down told Muldoon the whole story of how

Beaumont wanted to get back at his wife's affair with Gregorian at the same time rejuvenate his stalled career he felt sure a change in government would provide him.

At first Muldoon stared at her in disbelief until the full impact of what he had heard fully sank into his consciousness, gasping, "My God I've been had by that miserable bastard Beaumont! Does anyone else know about this?"

"Possibly his wife, she might know something about the career planning side of it. I was pretty mad at Nick dumping me for her, I never believed he'd be killed because of what we did." She finished, crying.

Touching her shoulder trying to comfort her saying it wasn't her fault, wouldn't have happened if they'd been honest in the first place. After she settled down they quickly left not finishing their meal. Back at his office he began feverishly writing the story, wondering if his paper would publish it?

Returning to his apartment early in the evening, Tony discovered a message on his phone's answering machine, it was from Anne asking him to call which excitedly did, she telling him at the constant urging of her mother had decided to return home for a last chance at saving their marriage, arriving the afternoon of the following day, Muldoon preparing to spend the rest of the night cleaning up before the happy event. As he was working, mulled over what he had learned from the Wilson meeting. The more he thought about it the more it made sense, aware that Beaumont and his wife had separated, his affair with Rowena Butler the probable cause, but would Carole Beaumont speak to him? He decided calling her.

The voice answering wasn't Carole's, it belonged to Pamela Masters, her mother, having accompanied her daughter on her return to Ottawa as a supporter while Carole settled the business over her husband's estate. "Hello, Carole?"

"No, it's Pamela Masters her mother. Whose speaking ?"

"It's Tony Muldoon. Please tell her it's very important that I speak to her." As she put the phone down, Muldoon could hear muffled voices in the background, finally heard the phone being picked up.

The cold, impersonal voice answering was Carole Beaumont's, "Yes Tony, why is it so important that we should speak, haven't you done enough damage already?"

Begging her to be patient, quickly told her the whole story of her husband's role in the leaked documents, not revealing how he learned this, Carole responded saying, she had suspected this might be the case. When Muldoon followed up asking if she had any knowledge of how he so quickly got his Deputy Minister appointment. After being assured anything he wrote would not make any reference to her involvement with Gregorian or to Scott's rumored affair with Rowena Butler, confided she overheard a late night conversation between her husband and a member of the Prime Minister's Office, who seemed aware Beaumont may have had something to do with the press leak, telling him his service to the government would be remembered by appointment for him. Promising faithfully not to reveal her identity, thanked Carole.

Hanging up, clapping his hands Muldoon shouted to the empty room, "Now I've got it all. What a story!" In his study, sitting behind his typewriter revising his article to 'The Making of a Government Mandarin, Scott Beaumont', for Muldoon, this was his payback time!

Muldoon's afternoon meeting with his wife at the railway station, although not warm, was cordial. That evening taking her out for dinner at a nearby restaurant, sitting at an isolated corner table, told her the entire story of what had transpired the previous day, able to mention Scott Beaumont's name for the first time not enraged doing so since Anne's involvement with him. Pleasantly surprised at her positive reaction to what she had just heard. They left holding hands, returned to their apartment, he eagerly showing her the article he had written.

After reading it, Anne commented, "It's very good Tony, not very complimentary to the new government. Do you think the paper will print it?"

"They'd better!" he replied grimly.

The next morning, bursting excitedly into his editor's office with the article on Beaumont clutched in his hand, exclaimed, "Jack do I ever have a great story for the paper!"

"Simmer down Tony or you'll blow gasket. What's got you so excited?" a smiling Thornton replied, sitting back in his chair sucking on his pipe.

"I know where the Braxton Gregorian leak came from and why!" Muldoon told his startled editor handing his article to read.

After carefully reading it, a worried looking Thornton asked, "Are you sure of your facts Tony?"

Surprised by his editor's glum expression, Muldoon responded, "Dead sure. What's wrong Jack, there's a hell of a great story here!"

"Maybe, Tony, but a number of senior influential political people in addition to Beaumont could be hurt here."

"I don't know who you're talking about, as for Beaumont he deserves to be exposed for prostituting the political process for his own selfish ends already causing the death of one man. Well Jack, are we going to print it?"

"I don't know about that, it's very explosive, I'll have to check it with Mister Marsden before going any further."

That afternoon, Muldoon and Thornton were called to report to the Publisher's office, Mister Marsden greeting them coldly, pointing to Muldoon's article on his desk asking him the same questions posed by Thornton, "Muldoon are absolutely sure of your facts, your sources, their reliability? Who are your sources?"'

"As far as the reliability of my sources, absolutely, their information checks out, as for their identity I gave my solemn word I wouldn't reveal it."

"Well Muldoon, we're not going to print it, and if I were you I'd forget all about it."

"Why not sir, it's a great story!"

"Never mind Muldoon, forget it, I have my reasons. Besides, I don't believe revealing the questionable behavior of one man worth embarrassing the government, surely there are other substantial issues for you to write about. You have a promising career in the newspaper business, I strongly advise you not to throw it away, forget this Beaumont business. That's all, when you leave ask my secretary to come in."

On entering, Marsden handed her Tony's article, saying gruffly, "Put this in the shredder."

Leaving Marsden's office a distressed Muldoon looking at a frowning Jack Thornton,

"Jack, he can't be serious wanting to shelve a story like this?"

"I'm afraid he is Tony." Thornton replied growing silent until reaching his office asking Tony to stay, closing his door. A very agitated Muldoon, starting to protest was silenced by his editor,

"Sit down Tony and be quiet for a moment. There's something you'd better understand about the publisher of our paper, he's not going allow a printing of anything that in any way could get John Braxton of the hook or embarrass the Conservative government. I assure you he meant everything he said . Look Tony, go home, be with your wife for the rest of the day, I'm sure you have a lot to talk about and for heaven's sake don't do anything that could screw everything up for yourself." Not replying, shaking his head Muldoon left for home.

Arriving at his apartment, he found his wife tidying up, surprised at his early homecoming, alarmed at the dejected look on her husband's face, cried out, "Tony! What happened? Is it me?"

"Oh heavens no, dear, it's not you, I'm so happy and thankful you're back, I've missed you so, I love you so much."

"I love and missed you too, you big dumb Irishman!" threw her arms around his neck kissing him passionately, without another word went to bed making love in a manner they hadn't done for some time. Later, over coffee, he told his sympathetic wife what had transpired in Marsden's office.

When he finished asked her, "What should I do Hon?"

"I don't know, dear, what can you do the paper refusing to print your story? What other options do you have?"

"I could go to the Liberals, no, I don't believe they would want any part in raising this mess again, not after what they've just gone through, on second thought, perhaps Jake Enright the new leader of the New Democratic Party might be interested."

"Maybe so Tony, it will mean your job!"

"I know dear, I just can't sit back and let Beaumont get away with this." he replied feeling miserable.

"No you can't!" Anne affirmed, "Why don't you see if you can see Enright, he may be glad to meet with you having no reason to protect the Tories or the Liberals."

"That's exactly what I'm going to do. I'll try to get hold of Enright tomorrow."

CHAPTER 27

Muldoon and Jake Enright - 'Payback Time'

The following morning, Muldoon called Enright's office, learning he was at a meeting, left a message asking him to call him on an urgent matter.

Phil Donner stopping by Tony's desk looked at him inquisitively, "You look troubled Tony, story not going well?"

"Phil, it's going just fine, I still have to clear up a few details." he nervously replied.

"Well Tony, staring at an empty typewriter won't help much. I'm going for a coffee, want to come along?"

"No thanks Phil, I have to stick around, I'm expecting a call." Donner no sooner left when his phone rang, it was Jake Enright returning his call. Tony looking around, ensuring he couldn't be overheard, speaking guardedly, "Hello, this is Tony Muldoon of the Tribune. I'd like to meet with you to discuss something important."

"I see, can you give me any idea what it's all about?"

"No, Mister Enright not over the phone."

"Okay, how about this afternoon at five in my office at the House?"

Thinking for a moment at meeting the NDP leader in such a public place, said to himself, "Why not? After all as a reporter it's my job to meet with such people. Yes Mister Enright I'll be there at five."

Tony called Anne, "Well, I've done it, I'm meeting Enright at five pm."

"That's fine Tony, I'm proud of you, I'll say a prayer."

"Thanks, I'll need it, I'll call you as soon as it's over. You know what this means Anne, I'll be finished with the paper!"

"I know dear, Scott must be stopped after what he's done to all of us. Don't worry, together we'll manage."

Muldoon, still apprehensive, carefully put a folded copy of his article in his jacket's inner pocket decided going to the Press Club for a drink, giving him time to think, before meeting with the NDP leader.

Jake Enright's office, frugal compared to the offices of Tory and Liberal leaders, papers, books, files spread everywhere, tall, young, wearing glasses, Enright with a searching analytical mind and a lawyers penchant for minute detail. A bachelor, he worked tirelessly reviewing the background of every major issue confronting the government, his advisors selected for their intelligence, capacity for hard work and long hours. Although leader of the New Democratic Party for only a short time, established a reputation for thinking clarity and notable perception during Question Period in the House. Although a thorn in the side of the former Prime Minister, Donald Porter, he was more like a spear for Grant Talbot's. Enright disliking the Tories intensely for what he considered to be their lack of a social conscience for the little man and the under privileged, strongly resented having to support them in defeating what he considered to be an impossibly corrupt government.

Enright originally planned to follow in the footsteps of his father, a distinguished Canadian diplomat and life-long Liberal supporter, all that changed after spending three years at the London School of Economics receiving his doctorate, then teaching economics at the University of Toronto. Immersed in what he considered to be a crying need for major economic and social reform in Canada, joined the NDP becoming elected its leader on the day of his thirty fifth birthday.

Arriving at Enright's office precisely at five, Tony found him sitting behind his desk in shirt sleeves engrossed in one of the files littering his desk. Seeing Tony enter the outer office, through his open door, got up motioning Muldoon to enter. Warmly shaking his hand, seated him in one of the two worn leather chairs in the corner beside a window,

"We've met before Mister Muldoon." he said, smiling, endeavoring putting his obviously discomfited visitor at ease.

"Yes we have Mister Enright, after a panel discussion at a regional development conference at the Chateau Laurier three months ago."

"Yes, that's right. I liked the way you treated the conference in your article particularly of some of the remarks I made." he replied, laughing. "Please excuse all the mess, now what is the urgent matter you wanted to discuss with me?"

Finding it difficult to start, Tony began with vague truisms, such as the need for political morality in government, the importance of identifying and reporting of unacceptable acts of political immorality as a matter of duty and conscience. Enright sensing something important was coming, listened patiently nodding his head in agreement with some of the universal truths

Tony was stating. When he finally got to the point of his visit, sweating profusely, told Enright of what he had learned about Scott Beaumont's role in the defeat of the Liberal government handing him the copy of his article.

After reading it, intently looking at Tony, remarked, "What you have told me and written, extremely interesting, even compelling but why are you telling me all about this? Surely your paper will be printing it?" Enright paused, waiting for Muldoon's answer,

"They won't Mister Enright absolutely refusing to report anything derogatory that may affect the Tory government, that's why I've come to you." he replied bitterly. "I was hoping you'd consider the matter of sufficient importance to raise in the house, then reported to the Public by a more politically open minded press than the Tribune."

Thinking carefully before replying, "I see. Now Mister Muldoon, please don't take offense, how can I be sure of the authenticity of your information? The charges in your article are very serious!"

"Because Mister Enright it means my job, the reliability of my sources, impeccable."

Enright looking out the window beside his chair paused, thinking, turned facing Tony, "Look Mister Muldoon, this is political dynamite, I must discuss it with some of my people, if they agree as I'm sure they will, I'll do it, raising it in the House during Question Period as a matter of privilege."

Muldoon relieved asked, "Will it take long for a decision?"

"No, I should be able to clear the matter up later this evening. By the way you wrote some of John Braxton's speeches didn't you?"

"Yes, nearly all the last ones he made."

"Good, they were excellent perhaps you can help me with this one?"

"Yes, of course."

Enright rising from his chair, waited for Tony to stand put his arm around the shorter man's shoulder saying, "Mister Muldoon I fully realize this has been a hard thing for you to do and the price you are prepared to pay, I admire you for doing it. Where can I reach you later?"

Giving Enright his home phone number, Muldoon quickly left, feeling relieved, wanting to see his wife, anxiously waiting for her husband's return. Later that evening, Enright called giving Tony the go ahead preparing his speech.

The following three days were frantic for Tony feigning illness at the office allowing time for him to help draft Enright's address to the House to be focused on the revelation of Beaumont's actions prior to the recent election. He worked at home during the day and with Enright in his modest Sandy Hill apartment late into the night until the NDP leader was satisfied with their joint effort.

Folding his speech putting it in a large brown envelope, smiling, waving it at Muldoon saying, "Well Tony this is it! I'll be raising it at tomorrow's Question Period in the House."

Later at home Tony and Anne were excitedly discussing Enright's forthcoming address, when the phone rang, picking it up he felt a cold chill hearing the voice on the other end, it was an agitated Phil Donner, Tony, what in the hell is going on? We've just learned that Jake Enright is going to blow the lid off the Gregorian affair again and you're involved?"

A nervous Muldoon replied, "Phil who in hell told you that?"

"Never mind, is it true?"

"I won't answer that !" Muldoon replied defensively.

"Well suite yourself. Thornton is mad as hell, if I were you I'd call him explaining yourself." Donner hung up.

Looking worried, Tony returned to the living to Anne who had overheard his part of the conversation.

"Trouble Tony?"

"Yes, I'm afraid so, Anne. Someone in Enright's office must have said something, anyways the cat's out of the bag, the paper knows."

The following afternoon, arriving at the House, taking his place in the Press gallery, obvious the word was out on Enright's forthcoming address, the gallery and spectator seats completely filled, Thornton and Donner looking grim, staring hard at Muldoon. Not looking back he searched the lower reaches to see if Beaumont was present found Scott sitting directly under him, as he looked down Beaumont looked up seeing Muldoon, their eyes meeting briefly, Scott turning his head away.

As soon as the Speaker of the house took his seat, Enright rose, requesting to address the House on a matter of privilege which was given. In a clear precise voice, speaking for nearly twenty minutes to a hushed house, scarcely glancing at his copious notes, in effect accused the Conservative government of rewarding a senior pubic official for betraying the trust of his government for personal gain, their behavior no better than that of the previous government.

After finishing, Enright sat down to resounding cheers from his party members, cat calls from the Conservatives, only a dead silence from the stunned Liberals, Rowena Butler left the House desperately holding back her tears, Scott Beaumont had left. When a disconsolate Grant Talbot returned to his office, Scott Beaumont's resignation lay on his desk. Enright's address was a nationally published triumph for his party, a destructive commentary on the questionable behavior of the other two.

On returning to the Tribune office, Muldoon found Thornton waiting for him, his desk cleared, his personal effects in a cardboard box. Thornton unsmilingly handed Muldoon a severance check, frowning, "Muldoon, you're through here, I doubt any other newspaper will touch you after that you've just done."

A security guard escort Muldoon out of the building. As he left carrying his box, said ruefully, "Yes I'm paying the price but at least I feel clean."

Doubting Thornton's dire threat his having no future in the business was valid, fully confident his established reputation as a news man, his recognized speech writing ability, perhaps even writing a book, there was no limit to the possibilities for him, Tony continued walking home anxious to see Anne.

EPILOGUE

Scott Beaumont wasn't out of work for very long after his resignation or concerned about money, receiving a generous settlement from the government, moved into a comfortable furnished apartment overlooking the driveway bordering the Ottawa river. He met discretely with Rowena Butler still loving him despite his government career ending by the Enright revelation. Avoiding the press, Butler returned to her Vancouver riding, fearing the worst from her supporters, elated learning she was still highly regarded, information quickly passed back to the Ottawa Conservative power brokers, and Grant Talbot, by the resourceful Peter Savage.

On returning, she met Beaumont at her cottage her face beaming, kissing him passionately, exclaiming, "Do I ever have good news for both of us"

"Good news? Well out with it sweetheart." Scott demanded eagerly, pulling her on his lap,

"Well, first of all I'm still in solid with my riding members almost unanimous in supporting me, the PM was very happy to learn this, it saved my job in Cabinet. Just wait until I tell you the rest."

Scott impatiently interjected, "Yes, yes go on Rowena."

"How would you like to be President of Allied Electronics in Toronto at three hundred and fifty thousand dollars a year with generous stock options?"

"You're putting me on!" he responded dubiously.

"No I'm not. I spoke to the Chairman, a strong party supporter, originally from Vancouver, in the city on family matters, told me he was looking for a bright young man for the job so I told him about you. He and some of his directors would like to meet with you when he returns to Toronto next week. Are you interested dear?"

"Yes, of course."

"Good, I'll let him know before I leave to attend an economic conference in the UK. I should be back a week Sunday giving you time for your meeting in Toronto. I have all the relevant detail for that meeting in my brief case. Let's stop talking and make love," she murmured, unbuttoning his shirt.

Scott Beaumont was ecstatic jogging the following early morning, at a steady pace along the pathway bordering the river bank, muttering to himself, "I'll show Muldoon and those other bastards they can't beat me! I've just collected two years salary, the Toronto job a one hundred percent pay raise with lots of perks, to hell with the government!"

Scott suddenly became aware of a sweat-suited man jogging behind starting to pass him, swarthy, short, stocky with powerful legs, smiling as he went by, Beaumont paying no attention to him. Much to his surprise, the same runner turned up at the same time the following morning, catching up jogged beside him for a few minutes until Scott sprinted ahead leaving his sweating companion far behind. The next day, Scott the only runner in the area, searched in vain for his silent companion, disappointed at not seeing him, suddenly saw the grey sweat-suited jogger running down the grassy slope to his right cutting onto the path behind him, slowed down to let the jogger catch up to him, planning to stop, finding out who he was on reaching large clump of bushes around a corner just ahead, now at a walking pace, hearing loud footsteps behind, started to turn his head to greet his unknown companion, felt a sharp snap around his neck, nothing more.

FLASH

'The body of a well known former senior government official was found this morning in a clump of bushes near the Parkway driveway. Preliminary indications are he was strangled with either a rope or a wire. The RCMP and the Ottawa police are investigating........'

Tony Muldoon found little satisfaction in Scott Beaumont's shocking violent end speculating correctly with Inspector Guthrie of the RCMP, likely part of a final settling of accounts by the drug Syndicate. Cathy Wilson mysteriously disappeared, ending up a name in the Ottawa police register of missing persons. At first Muldoon felt some guilt of his role in revealing what Beaumont had done, quickly put it out of his mind, getting on with his life, having managed to save his marriage with Anne. Helped by Jake Enright, Tony received some lucrative speech writing contracts, outlined an idea for a political intrigue novel, favorably reviewed by a book publisher prompted him to write it.

Unknown to him at this time, Jake Enright, convinced the Tory government would soon fall, certain the Canadian people, fed up with the shocking practices of the two traditional parties, would turn to a NDP party running on a government reform ticket, felt Muldoon might be an ideal reform candidate for an Ottawa west riding.

Meanwhile, encouraged by his wife, Tony sat down at his typewriter, a glass of scotch close by, began to write,

'The Mandarin'

'A Mandarin was a high official of China under the Empire; the nine classes of Mandarin were distinguished from one another by a certain type of jewel button worn on the cap.'

I first met Scott Beaumont.............

The End

PART 2
The Syndicate

'The puppets bowing, gyrating to the puppet master's
tightly controlled pull on their strings.'

CHAPTER 1

Boris Aristine 'The Immigration Fix'

Boris Aristine a powerful but pictorially virtually unrecognized major European drug dealer, never having been charged or formally photographed by the French police, who along with the Interpol investigating the drug operations they suspected were being carried out under the cover of his commercially successful cosmetic import-export business centered in Paris. Having failed in a previous attempt transferring the control of his operations to Canada, arranged a settling of accounts, a death sentence, for those considered responsible for its failure. Deciding on a new approach, changing his identity including minor cosmetic changes, Aristine awaited his trusted eyes and ears in Montreal and Ottawa, federal government, well connected lawyer Jean Dubois.

On arriving at Aristine's ornate expensively furnished office, Dubois was ushered in by Jorge Manoff, a Macedonian boyhood friend of Aristine, formerly a hired assassin now his personal protector and enforcer. After a cordial handshake Aristine inviting Dubois to take a seat in the lounge area asking Manoff to arrange for a drink for his very nervous looking visitor.

"Well Jean from your last telegram I assume you have good news for me."

"Yes Mister Aristine, very good news! When I informed my government contacts the huge amount of money you were prepared to invest establishing a cosmetic import- export business in Montreal and the number of new jobs to be created, an approval normally taking six months was accomplished in six weeks! Also a new identity has been created for you and Jorge. You are now David Rosanoff and Jorge, Ted Cristoff with all the paperwork and procedures involved, done."

"Excellent Jean. Another prime example of when there's enough money, anything can be bought. You won't be unhappy with the reward for your good efforts. Now let's get down to business, tell me what is going on in Montreal, Toronto an d New York? I gathered from your carefully guarded comments over the phone there are problems?"

looking appreciatively at the trim more youthful appearing, ruggedly handsome figure seated opposite him, Dubois replied, "Yes Mister Aris... No, I mean Mister Rosanoff. We'd better get used to using your new name. There are problems. New York is stable under Julius Silverberg's firm hand. Montreal fine except Frankie Gianni's concerns over some of the moves in his direction Joey Palermo seems to be making from Toronto. The Ottawa political scene is in a shambles with the Conservative government managing only slim minority in the recent election, now dependent on the support of its new opposition a resurging National Democratic Party.

The Canadian Mounties have stopped their intensive

investigation of the Gregorian and Beaumont deaths although suspecting, finding no connection to the Syndicate in Montreal. Another problem, a woman, was quietly taken care of with no police reaction, however we could use a closer presence on the Ottawa scene re-establishing connections with senior level government members."

"Well Jean, I've already decided to establish myself in Ottawa not Montreal avoiding being connected with Gianni, however I want you to get professional help locating someone capable of supervising the establishment of the cosmetic business there as well as managing it. Also, for making productive government contacts, reopening the Oasis, hiring someone suitable to manage it, not the former one,"

A very worried looking Jean Dubois replying, " Mister Rosanoff, do you think your moving to Ottawa reopening the Oasis, wise? Why not Toronto? Remember the Gregorian Ottawa experience!"

Enraged, Rosanoff replied, "Look Dubois, I'm not Niccolo Gregorian. I never want to hear that name mentioned again, is that clear?"

"Perfectly clear." a profusely sweating alarmed Dubois replied seeing the menacing figure of the now renamed Jorge Manoff lurking in the background.

A softer toned Rosanoff responding, "Well Jean, I think you'd better return to Montreal as soon as possible. There's still a great deal of arranging to be done." Nodding at Cristoff,"Take Mister Dubois to the airport in my limousine and see he gets the earliest flight possible back to Montreal" Shaking hands with a trembling Dubois,, "Jean, check with my secretary on the way out, she has something for you."

Dubois, immensely relieved as he boarded his aircraft with Cristoff watching him from the passenger boarding exit, seated alone at the back of the first class section, after take- off, opened the envelope given to him by Rosanoff's secretary, inside a hundred thousand dollar bank note made out to him. Heaving a sigh of relief put the envelope carefully in his suit coat's inside pocket.

Rosanoff, a committed bachelor, musing after Dubois departed, "Yes, Nicky Gregorian with his insatiable appetite for women, especially his last one, was an almost fatal error. I should have paid more attention to the Ottawa situation."

CHAPTER 2

Carole Beaumont

Carole Beaumont, while setting her deceased husband's affairs in Ottawa decided to sell her Georgian Manor home to the Muldoon's. Tony, now a Member of Parliament and a rising star in the New Democratic Party, his recently published book 'The Mandarin', a literary and financial success. Against her mother, Pamela Masters' wishes decided to stay, taking over her ruthlessly murdered husband's luxury apartment, enabling her to reconnect with her friends, Paula and Craig Johnson of the Privy Council Office, steadfastly supportive during the unleashing of the "Gregorian Affair' scandal and its devastating aftermath.

Left financially comfortable by her husband, Carole was trying to decide on how to be constructively busy. She was presented with an opportunity while lunching alone at the Chateau enjoying its air conditioned ambience, a relief from the mid July heat. Also lunching alone at a nearby table, Jane Price, owner of the successful trendy 'Fashion Place' boutique, spotting Carole remembered selling her an expensive cocktail dress in the past, came over introducing herself. Recalling their earlier meeting at her shop, Carole invited Jane joining her for lunch during which they carefully confined their conversation to vague generalities, avoiding any embarrassing comment about the past.

Jane, sipping on a martini, asked by Carole as to the state of her business, answered, "Business has not only been great but too great, in fact I need to expand. A store next door to me is becoming available, taking it over joining it to mine will require a fairly heavy investment of capital in construction and inventory beyond my means so I'm thinking of looking for a partner willing to invest in it."

Carole sipping on a champagne cocktail, obviously interested asked quietly, "A partner Jane, on what terms?"

"I'd say ownership. An equal share in the business. Say Carole, if you're interested come with me to the shop after we finish our lunch, I'll show you what I have in mind, it's not far from here."

"Yes I know Jane, it's in a great location. I'm ready whenever you are."

Walking along the Spark's Street Mall, an odd looking pair, Jane, short, full figured, perky, bubbly, dark haired, pretty rather than beautiful; Carole, statuesque, blonde, breath-taking figure, stunningly attractive, both tastefully dressed, caught the eyes of the men walking by them. After looking over Jane's plans for expanding her business operation Carole contacted her lawyer who had a business development specialist examine the Fashion Place's operation, its books, plan for expansion, deciding it to be a worthwhile investment. Jane Price agreeing, their lawyers drew up an agreement, Carole established as joint owner of the business, working with Jane two days during the week and Saturdays. Jane patiently 'showed her the ropes' in the sales end of the business as well as inventory management. Carole found it interesting and challenging.

Over the next few months, the partners developed a comfortable personal relationship. Jane, a divorcee after an unhappy marriage, wary of any serious involvement with men, enjoyed an occasional night out 'clubbing' after work on a Saturday. Carol confined herself to regular 'get-togethers' with the Johnson's either at their home or at her apartment until on a Tuesday in the late fall, while the Johnson's were on a European vacation, was asked by Jane if she would like to join her in a visit to a club after work the following Saturday. A little restless, bored by a lack of any night-life, agreed until learning it was to be the recently re- opened Oasis. Price unaware of Carole's tempestuous relationship with its previous owner, Nick Gregorian ruthlessly murdered earlier in the year.

Surprised at Carole's adamant refusal, "For heaven's sake Carole, why not? I've met its new owner David Rosanoff, a perfect gentleman and not bad looking."

"No Jane, absolutely not and that's final!"

Jane taken aback by Carole's angry response, "Well you don't have to bite my head off. I thought it might be a nice change for you after all you've been through."

In a more conciliatory tone Carole apologizing, "I'm sorry Jane, you didn't deserve that, maybe somewhere else another time."

Later in the week after reading a flattering account of the Oasis and its new owner, her curiosity aroused, approached her partner, "Jane if you'll forgive my rudeness and still want me to, I'll join you Saturday night."

"That's great Carole, you won't regret it."

Turning away from Jane, still failing driving out of her mind the intense sexual awakening Nick Gregorian had created in her inner being, the months of anguished despair she felt after his violent death. Although unaware she was about to meet the man responsible for ordering the murders of both her lover and husband, intuitively murmured under her breath, "I'm not so sure about that!"

CHAPTER 3

Carole Meets David Rosanoff

David Rosanoff sat at his secluded table giving him a unobstructed view of the entrance, discussing Oasis business with his manager. On seeing Jane Price entering with a stunningly beautiful exquisitely dressed tall statuesque blond stood up waving them over to his table. Carole hesitated, remembering her visit the first night meeting Nick Gregorian, the champagne, music, dancing, her intense sexual awakening, their unrestricted passionate love-making. Taking hold of herself she followed Jane over to the table where a smiling Rosanoff now alone, waited. She agreed with Jane's assessment of him, ruggedly good looking, even handsome.

After a firm handshake and introduction, Rosanoff seated them saying to himself, "So this is the Carole Beaumont that so infatuated Niccolo. Now I understand!" a magnum of Champagne chilling in a ice bucket was quickly brought to them, after filling their glasses, Rosanoff, sensing Carole's quiet, sad reserve, opening the conversation, "I understand from Jane that you are a business partner of hers Missis Beaumont; if that striking ensemble you are wearing so delightfully is an example of your line of women's wear you must be doing a very good business indeed."

"That's very complimentary Mister Rosanoff, I owe it all to Jane's excellent taste and fine business sense. I'm still learning."

Jane Price intervened, "Since I'm Jane don't you think we should change the Missis and Mister to Carole and David?"

"Yes, by all means." both agreed.

For the remainder of the evening their conversation was restricted to pleasant generalities, including a mutual interest of Carole and David in classical music especially in Tchaikovsky's ballet compositions. Initially, Carole felt uncomfortable, her memories of her nights there with Gregorian unsettling her; as the evening wore on, the champagne, music, sound of laughter from the young crowd members enjoying themselves, lessened her guilty feeling, finding David Rosanoff to be a congenial pleasant host. The women leaving shortly after midnight after a cordial handshake, David saying he hoped they would return soon for another visit, Jane quickly saying yes, Carole non committal.

Jane drove Carole to where she normally parked her car while at their store, asked, "Well Carole what did you think?"

"Of the evening? I found it quite pleasant."

"No, I mean of him?"

"He seems nice enough. Who was the man standing in the background all evening?"

"Oh that's Ted Cristoff, a sort of a personal assistant, he's always with him ."

Monday morning they were interrupted by the arrival of a dozen red roses for each of them along with a written invitation by Rosanoff for a return visit. In the morning the following Saturday,

Carole was surprised seeing a smiling nattily dressed David Rosanoff entering the shop, Ted Cristoff waiting patiently outside by Rosanoff's parked limousine.

Approaching Carole, signaling Jane Price to join them, explained his unexpected presence, "I know this is very short notice, if you don't have anything planned, how would the two of you like to attend the National Arts Center's orchestra's classical evening tonight featuring Tchaikovsky's Sleeping Beauty Suite?"

Jane replied, "Thank you David, not me, I'm not really into classics." turning t Carole, "How about you? The classics are more your thing."

"I don't know. There's so little time to get ready after work." she replied.

"Nonsense!" Rosanoff said, "Take the rest of the day off, it looks like a quiet day here. You'll enjoy it." Then added, "Yes, I'm sure you will, say yes and I'll pick you up at seven thirty."

Carole hesitated momentarily, replied, "Oh very well, yes."

After Receiving Carole's Parkway drive address and phone number, a pleased looking David Rosanoff left, leaving a very unsure Carole Beaumont wondering if she was making a big mistake, quickly dismissed it from her mind, left, to have her hair done.

Rosanoff and his chauffer, Ted Cristoff, picked her up. When they arrived at the National Arts Center just before the start of the concert, Carole was surprised that Cristoff wordlessly accompanied them into the Center.

Rosanoff smiled and explained, "Since your friend Jane decided not to join us, I told Ted he could use the extra ticket. He has a taste for good music,

Carole was skeptical, but as she sat between the men noted that Cristoff truly enjoyed the music. He applauded heartily at the concert's finale.

Leaving the Arts Center, standing at the entrance chatting excitedly about the concert, waiting for Cristoff and the limousine. After the car's arrival she politely declined her escort's offer to take her to the Oasis for an after concert drink, asking to be driven home.

On arriving, after they warmly shook hands she said, "David, the concert was very enjoyable, thank you."

"We must d this again Carole."

"That would be nice David" she replied invitingly.

The following morning, Carole received a special Sunday delivery of an outstandingly beautiful flower bouquet with a note 'A beautiful remembrance for a beautiful lady. Thank you for a wonderful evening. David.'

CHAPTER 4

The Courtship

During the following weeks Carole politely refused Rosanoff's dinner invitations finally agreeing to meet him at the Chateau dining room on a late September Saturday evening. Surprised at how pleased she felt seeing him again, was relieved by the apparent absence of Ted Cristoff.

While enjoying an after dinner cognac she informed him, "David, I've decided to revert to maiden name, Masters as soon as my lawyer can arrange it."

"Ah, Masters! That is a nice name, Carole. If you run into any problems, let me know, my lawyers will ensure it is accomplished quickly." Rosanoff replied in a voice of a man accustomed to authority.

During the following weeks they met regularly, usually on a Saturday evening, dining at a restaurant, occasionally at the Oasis, Carole finally feeling comfortable there. Their frequent meetings only interrupted by his never explained 'business' trips to Montreal, occasionally Toronto and New York, always accompanied by

Cristoff. Now Carole Masters, she invited him for a Sunday dinner at her apartment to celebrate her name change.

Jane, on learning of Carole's dinner invitation laughingly commented," This must be getting serious. Now you're out showing him you can cook!"

"Don't be silly Jane. he's only a friend." she replied blushing.

Price staying silent remembering the last time she had heard the 'only a friend' remark.

After dinner, on leaving, Rosanoff tried to take Carole in his arms.

She firmly pushed him away, "No David I'm not ready for that!"

A week later, while Rosanoff was away on a business trip to Montreal and New York, Carole's mother arrived for a visit, pleased at her daughter reverting to her maiden name. One evening, while helping her daughter send the name change to appropriate recipients, asked Carole about the man she was seeing, only having been given a brief description, not his name.

After an early supper she asked, "Now Carole, tell me about this considerate man you've been seeing. You've said very little about him in our phone conversations, not even his name."

"Yes Mother, he is very kind and considerate, intelligent, enjoys good music, he's excellent company."

"Carole, his name, tell me his name." her mother demanded.

Hesitating momentarily, knowing of her mother's bitter racial bias against foreigners, replied sighing resignedly, "Rosanoff, David Rosanoff."

"Oh my God, a Russian, you're seeing a Russian!"

"No Mother he's not a Russian, he's Macedonian and Greek."

"Good Lord! That's worse! Haven't you learned anything from your disastrous affair with that Italian? It's a disgrace to our family. Oh how I wish you hadn't changed you name back to Masters!'

Sobbing bitterly, went to bed, returning to Toronto the following morning. Many weeks passed before she would speak to her daughter.

During the following months, their relationship affectionately warmer, Carole agreed to accompany Rosanoff on a weekend trip to the renowned Quebec resort hotel, The Chateau Montebello. On the understanding they would have separate suites, were driven there by the ever watchful Cristoff, whose almost continuous presence now accepted by Carole.

After a delicious dinner, while savoring a cognac and music from soft jazz quartet, looking directly at her partner Carole asked, "You know David after these many months I know so little about you,, although it's obvious to me you're someone of significance."

Putting down his goblet, looking at her intently, Rosanoff answered, "Carole, let me put it this way. In my culture we rigidly separate business affairs from family affairs. However, I'm involved in a number of business enterprises including my cosmetic import-export businesses in Paris and now in Montreal with branches in Toronto and New York."

Laughing she replied, "Very impressive! Are you telling me you consider me to be family?"

"In a manner of speaking, yes! In my business men of influence and power often make enemies that's why Ted Cristoff is nearly always with me, not only a loyal dedicated protector but a trusted boyhood friend from my country. I think this is all you need to know about me. Tomorrow I have a surprise for you we'll be leaving early driving to the Mont Tremblant area north of Montreal, so a good night's sleep would be wise."

Escorting Carole to her suite, departed for his after a tender goodnight kiss. She mulled over his business explanation, her mother's reaction to Rosanoff, realizing she was beginning to fall in love with this mysterious powerful man. Going to sleep, anxiously wondered, 'What on earth have I got myself involved in?'

Around noon the next day, approaching Quebec's famed ski area, Rosanoff pointed out to Carole a large imposing villa nestled in the side of one of the hills.

She asked. "What is it David, a small resort?"

"No, it's a private residence." he replied.

Surprised she responded, "Who could afford to own a place like that, do you know?"

"Yes I do." Rosanoff replied, smiling.

"Who?" she asked breathlessly, anticipating the answer.

"Me!"

Driving uphill along the winding road to the villa's entrance, met there by the three regular live -in staff members, the house keeper, cook and butler who carried Carole's and David's luggage into the house. Cristoff was taken to the comfortable staff quarters in a small residence in the back. An excited Carol, closely followed by David, entered his surprise, the recently purchased, completely renovated, magnificent country residence, by one of Montreal's premier interior decorators. After viewing the large downstairs drawing room, adjoining dining room, book-lined library and study, David led her upstairs on the broad winding stairway to a smaller richly furnished drawing room. At each end a large bedroom. Taking Carole to one on the left David opening its door smilingly invited her to enter.

The large room was completely decorated in a French, Marie Antoinette motif both walls and ceiling, an excellent life-size reproduction of her famous portrait on the wall behind a huge four poster bed. On a table on the far side of the room a record player and a collection of Chopin's music, then showed her the adjoining bathroom with a large sit in tub.

Overcome with emotion she exclaimed, "Oh David, this is all so magnificent."

Smiling he replied, "I'm so glad you like it because this is where you're going to sleep tonight and I hope on many more."

Not replying to his obvious inference asked, "And where are you going to sleep?"

"In the other bedroom off the other side of the drawing room, come, I'll show it to you."

Eagerly following him, led into an oak paneled bedroom decorated circa the Napoleonic era, with a striking life sized David portrait reproduction of that great leader hanging on the wall behind a sturdy bed. The rest of his furnishings simple, functional.

Left alone in her bedroom to tidy up, unpack her luggage she came to the shocking realization of why he had done all of this, it was for her! After unpacking, closed her door, took off her skirt and blouse, pulling back the pink flower decorated coverlet of the bed, lying on its pink satin sheets, wondering, "Was she really ready for this? Just who is this man she was falling in love with?" Later after an excellent dinner prepared by Helena the cook, served by a quiet, polite Roger the butler, she noticed he wore a shoulder holstered handgun under his jacket.

Seeing Carole's concerned look Rosanoff explained, "It's only for our protection and security." then quickly changing the subject, "Let's go into the drawing and listen to Chopin, especially to his 'Polonaise, dramatic, inspiring."

Finishing a second Grand Marnier after dinner aperitif, Carole yawned, apologizing, "David it's been a fantastic but long day. It's time for me to go to bed."

After Rosanoff dismissed the staff, they went up the stairs, the ever alert Cristoff quietly entering unnoticed to sit guard in the library. Reaching her bedroom David kissed her gently, about to leave she took him by the hand leading him inside, closing the door.

After a wonderful caring and sharing night of love-making with her new lover, followed by two carefree, idyllic days, on their last night, David asked her to share his life my moving into his awe inspiring villa, not mentioning marriage.

She, still unaware of his earlier deadly involvement in her life, replied, "You're asking a great deal of me David."

"Yes I am. Financially you will have no worries . I'll ensure you'll be very comfortably set for life before you move."

"David dear, I'll have to think this over."

"Of course Carole, please don't take too long. I'll be away most of next week, let me know when I return."

After Rosanoff returned, she did saying a resounding, "Yes!" unleashing the remaining pent up sexual passion she had been holding back, astounding a pleasantly surprised Rosanoff.

After completing his offered financial arrangements, Rosanoff arranged her move to his villa.

On arriving Carole worriedly asked herself, "What on earth am I doing! Have I just bargained myself?"

CHAPTER 5

The Toronto Syndicate -
Giuseppe 'Joey' Palermo

G iuseppe 'Joey' Palermo's grew up in the predominately post
World War 1 Italian district in Toronto's Manning and Euclid
Avenue area. The closely knit predominately Italian Catholic
families lived in rows of small semi-detached houses lining the
streets, the hard working adult men mainly employed as brick
layers and skilled cement workers. Their wives prided themselves
over the mouth watering aroma of their home baked bread, the
men, their often excellent home- made wine. On both sides of the
Palermo's lived the sisters of his mother, his cousins Salvatore 'Sal'
and Giovanni 'Johnny' Ricci on one side, their father Italian born,
cousins Rodolfo 'Rudy' and Carlo Braganzi on the other, their
father a Sicilian. Up the street close family friends, the Fossi's their
children, Pasqual 'Patsy', his younger sister, Angelina, 'Angie'. Next
door to them lived the local butcher's family, his son Jimmy Bonero,

a close friend of Joey Palermo. Directly across the street from them, the Saint Francis Catholic church and adjoining school.

At the bottom of Manning Avenue there was a drug store owned by the highly respected pharmacist, Victor Reardon, whose son Michael often spent his Saturdays at his father's store, over time becoming friends with Joey Palermo and his cousins, all appreciating his father's advice and help for their families. Michael, like his father, learned to speak a passable street Italian on weekends and holidays helping at his father's meetings with local fathers seeking advice from the educated pharmacist on a wide range of issues. Young Reardon often ushered them into his father's small business-like office in the basement of the store, accepting their gifts appreciation, fresh home-made bread, liters of domestic wine, Italian biscuits, always saying a polite 'Gracia' on his father's behalf, when they left. This often witnessed by their sons accompanying them. Despite his not being Italian, they eventually accepted young Reardon, 'The Irisher', as one of them.

The situation changed radically even tragically, when the economic devastating impact of the Dirty Thirties hit the community affecting nearly every family including Victor Reardon. Vainly trying to meet the increasing need for medicine by community members who couldn't afford to pay, eventually going bankrupt, losing his store, his upper middle class home in Toronto's upper-scale Kew Beach - Kingston Road area. The loss of their beautiful furniture witnessed by a shocked unknowing 9 year old Michael one day on returning from the progressive Kew Beach public school, seeing everything being loaded on a large truck. Some items permitted under a heartless Bankruptcy Law, such as bedding, his baby brother's crib, basic china-ware, cutlery, clothing, dumped unceremoniously on the side walk.

Shortly after the big truck left, a Manning Avenue friend, still managing keeping his old rattling small truck arrived, helping Michael's father load their effects on its back His distraught mother and baby brother sitting in the front, Michael and his father standing in the back, a few disturbed neighbors looked on as it drove away. They moved into a cold water two room flat above the now vacant drugstore, furnished only with a small battered table four chairs, cooking and heating provided by a small barrel shaped Quebec heater in the centre of the rug- less living room floor, in the only bedroom a decrepit spring double bed with a stained torn mattress.

Shortly after the Reardon's arrival, Manning Avenue neighbors appeared, the Palermo's, Ricci's, Braganzi's, the butcher Bonero, despite their own serious financial condition, with gifts of food, a bottle of wine, a salami chub, providing a cot for Michael to sleep in. Over time generously providing other items of necessary furniture, an ultimate example of caring and sharing. The Reardon's accepted as members of their closely knit community, Michael as a member of the Manning Avenue street gang headed by 13 year old Joey Palermo, 'The Enforcer'. Victor Reardon, shortly after as had so many other community members were compelled to do, experienced the humiliation of applying for City Welfare in order to pay his meager rent as well as put food on the table, in Manning Avenue parlance 'Go on the Pogie!'

Michael Reardon's entry into Joey Palermo's gang, uneventful, not asked to take part in their smash and grab operations, which even in his young mind he considered unproductive, often leading to arrests, their mothers' tearful pleads for leniency for their sons. Victor Reardon was often asked to intercede for them, he unaware that his son was also involved. It came to a head when Joey Palermo faced a two year term in Reform School, at Victor Reardon's and a Priest's intercession given one last chance. On another occasion released when a frightened injured night watchman refused to testify against him. Now really concerned, Joey swallowed his pride, reluctantly asked young Reardon for his advice.

Aware of Palermo's quick sometimes violent temper Michael reluctantly replied, "Well Joey, first of all you have to stop the smash and grab business, it will only be trouble for you and the others."

Palermo angrily responded, "So what do you suggest we do? We just can't sit back and do nothing! Taking it is the only way we can get anything."

"Change the way you're doing it. First of all better planning and how you do it, Joey."

"Ok Mikey what would you do?"

"First I'd look the place over then have some of the guys get the attention of the clerk or store keeper while others make the grab."

"How would you keep the clerk's attention?"

"Easy Joey, start a fight, knock something over that needs picking up."

It didn't take Palermo long following Reardon's suggestion, it worked like a charm earning Michael the title 'Maestro'. This technique not only succeeding then, also later in Palermo's criminal career by distracting the police's attention from the intended target by seemingly hitting another. Over the next two years, although Joey retained the nominal leadership of the gang it was young Reardon who actually ran the show resulting in no arrests, increasingly remunerative hits with no blood spilled, the members families not asking where the sudden affluence of their sons was coming from.

When trouble arose for the gang either internally or from the outside, Michael only had to say to Palermo, "Joey, take care of it!"

The combined leadership of Maestro and The Enforcer proved formidable, not unnoticed by outside major criminal interests, ending when Victor Reardon was employed as the manager of a north Toronto drug store moving his family to a comfortable apartment in the vicinity of the store, a considerable distance from Manning Avenue.

Joey taking full control, over the following years with the help of an outside major crime interest, built it into a powerful criminal operation consisting of gambling, money loan sharking, and escort services. He forced his smaller competitors buying his expensive protection services finally drugs. His multi- million dollar operation destined to become the Toronto Syndicate member of a major international crime organization headed by Boris Aristine in Paris. The drugs, primarily marijuana and cocaine, shipped by plane to Toronto and Montreal, from Jamaica or Costa Rica or to Halifax by ship from Guyana and the Dominican Republic then driven to Montreal and Toronto for distribution.

Michael Reardon's life moved into an entirely different direction, his pharmacist father started a real estate business on the side, beginning with houses, then small hotels. Helped by his wife, the business on the side so successful he gave up being a pharmacist creating the Orma Realty it soon becoming a major Toronto real estate operation. His family returned to the living level they had enjoyed prior to the destructive impact of the late depression.

For Michael, it meant a good high school, serving the last two years of the war the Canadian Army with service in Northwest Europe. After the war at University, participated in its Canadian Officers Training Corps commissioned at its end as a Lieutenant in the reserves. He served as an infantry officer during the Korean War, wounded, decorated, sent home with his best army friend also severely wounded. On their recovery, they entered his father's real estate business taking it over as partners on Victor Reardon's death.

Giuseppe Palermo's family's near catastrophic plight during the Great Depression, was heart-breaking. His mother frequently ailing, his father increasingly angry, at failing finding work, a proud Italian forced to apply for City welfare. A young, very resentful Joey taking to the streets, found stealing the only way getting something of value from an indifferent uncaring society. Helped by his cousins and the butcher's son, started by stealing from fruit and vegetable stands, then five and dime stores finally breaking and entry unto stores at night until discovered by a night watchman, beaten severely with a hammer by Palermo. Joey was arrested, quickly released, the frightened watchman refusing to identify him, a lesson not forgotten. It was at this point he sought the advice of a recent new gang member, Michael Reardon successfully changing his method of operation.

In the years following Reardon's departure, Palermo developed into a very successful, tall, muscular, good-looking even handsome young Italian openly admired by girls and young women, especially by his girlfriend since childhood, Angie Fossi, whom he made pregnant subsequently quickly marrying, as was the custom in his society. Wanting involvement in the increasingly lucrative drug market met secretly met with his Capo counterpart in Montreal, Francesco 'Frankie' Gianni, subsequently both joined the Aristine cartel, vowing to steer clear of each other's 'territory. . .

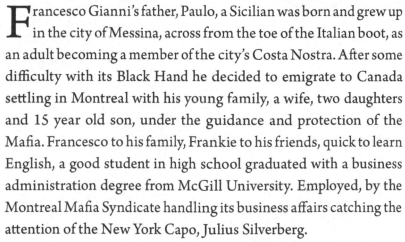

CHAPTER 6

The Montreal Syndicate
Francesco 'Frankie' Gianni

Francesco Gianni's father, Paulo, a Sicilian was born and grew up in the city of Messina, across from the toe of the Italian boot, as an adult becoming a member of the city's Costa Nostra. After some difficulty with its Black Hand he decided to emigrate to Canada settling in Montreal with his young family, a wife, two daughters and 15 year old son, under the guidance and protection of the Mafia. Francesco to his family, Frankie to his friends, quick to learn English, a good student in high school graduated with a business administration degree from McGill University. Employed, by the Montreal Mafia Syndicate handling its business affairs catching the attention of the New York Capo, Julius Silverberg.

Gianni, spent two years there organizing and managing that city's organization's business affairs, developing a comfortable relationship with its head man. Returning to Montreal assumed the leadership of the Montreal operation. Now in his mid forties, shrewd, 'business' oriented, quiet spoken, disarmingly ruthless when necessary, "Never stand in any dark corners if you've offended Frankie!" a not so funny jest among the organization's 'soldiers'.

After careful consideration, urged by Silverberg, who had allied himself with Aristine, Gianni decided to join the drug cartel, sent his lawyer, Jean Dubois to Paris to arrange his side of the agreement. At Silverberg's insistence raised it with his counterpart in Toronto, Joey Palermo, whom he didn't trust he not being Sicilian, or even Italian born.

CHAPTER 7

The New York Syndicate –
Julius Silverberg

Julius Silverberg, 'Big Julie', a name he hated, to some of his soldiers when out of his hearing, grew up on the East Side Jewish district of New York during the 'Prohibition Era,' created by the American Government's Volstead Act. The infamous 'Roaring Twenties,' featured the likes of Al Capone in Chicago, Lucky Luciano, Dutch Shultz and Myer Lasky, of Murder Incorporated infamy, in New York, a shocking period introducing the large scale illegal production and importation of alcohol. A number of Canadian alcohol and beer producing companies eager and willing suppliers sending by truck and motor launch to the huge fantastically profitable US market. Ships from England and Europe anchored outside the 20 mile limit, unloaded into smaller boats shipped to waiting trucks in smaller unwatched US ports. Gambling, loan sharking, prostitution, the numbers racket, murder for hire, complementing the highly profitable alcohol business, often resulted in gang rivalries fierce and deadly.

Silverberg's father Nathan, a poorly paid furrier, was brought into the New York operation by Lasky a family friend and member of the same synagogue, taking over the marketing and sales of significant amounts of expensive fur coats and other stolen merchandise. His considerably improved finances enabled sending his intelligent son Julius to New York University, graduating with a degree in business and finance. Subsequently employed by the organization as its business manager under Luciano's direction, years later rising to its head, the first Jewish Capo. Shrewd, calculating, now in his early 50's. Deceptively deadly, ruthless in business, was a loving, urbane family man to his wife and two daughters. A devout orthodox Jew, he never discussed business affairs with his family. His motto, Business is Business! Family is Family! Living in a discretely guarded estate outside of Grafton New Jersey commuted daily in his chauffeured bullet proofed limousine to his office in New York's business centre. Having more in common and comfortable with his Montreal counterpart, also with Boris Aristine's skillful strength in business affairs, not with Toronto's unpredictable often tempestuous, Joey Palermo.

Of the three North American Syndicate city heads, the only two having met Aristine before his identity change to Rosanoff were Gianni and Silverberg. As part of his identity change was Aristine's supposed retirement to an undisclosed location. Rosanoff identified as a close associate with Cosa Nostra approval, appointed in his place responsible moving the overall control of the Syndicate's European operations to Canada. Only Gianni and Silverberg, with Mafia trusted roots, made aware of the truth. On the pain of death they were sworn not to reveal it to anyone, a pledge faithfully kept.

CHAPTER 8

The Cosmetic Import -
Export Business-
Carole Masters Meets
Randolph Summers

In accordance with Aristine's now Rosanoff's instructions, a relieved resourceful Jean Dubois located a suitable plant housing a chemical laboratory testing facility, its prior business recently relocated to an economically distressed area in the southern United States. Using his significant Quebec political connections obtained considerable financial support from the Quebec government. He hired a young McGill University Business School graduate, recently earning a Harvard University Master's degree in Business Administration, Randolph 'Randy' Summers. Tall, athletically built, fine featured, dark brown wavy hair, hazel grey flecked eyes, a warm engaging smile, with French help set up the Montreal operation modeled along the same lines as the financially successful business in Paris under the watchful eye of Jean Dubois

Rosanoff, preoccupied with settling Carole Beaumont into his Mont Tremblant area villa, his lack of attention to business, concerned his Canadian and American Syndicate deputies becoming a major issue when Palermo set up drug sales contacts in the Western Quebec area bordering Ontario, the New York State area bordering Lake Ontario. The latter not yet a great concern to Julius Silverberg, the former of great concern to Frankie Gianni, Palermo having broken their business non-tampering agreement, both privately expressing their concerns to Rosanoff, at first receiving little reaction, infatuated with Carole Masters preoccupied settling and living with her in the Mont Tremblant mansion.

To allay any fears Carole still had over the legitimacy of his activities, Rosanoff decided to show her the now up and running Cosmetic business Montreal operation set up, effectively managed by Randolph Summers. After a short tour of the premises followed by the ever present Ted Cristoff, sat down to a catered lunch in Summers' oak paneled boardroom, a special table cloth covered table arranged for the purpose. Cristoff departed to the plant's cafeteria. During lunch, Carole, couldn't help comparing Randy, not to Rosanoff, but to Nicky Gregorian finding him a younger physically anglicized version of her brutally murdered former lover. Summers in turn found her to be the most beautiful woman he had ever met.

Rosanoff received a message from Gianni stressing the immediate importance of their having a meeting to discuss a serious business problem with Toronto. Unaware of the chemistry developing between the two, asked Summers to arrange Carole's transportation back to his villa. Kissing her left with Cristoff to meet with Gianni. Summers did not arrange her return to the villa, deciding to drive her there himself. During the long drive, immensely enjoyed each others' company.

On arriving awed by the imposing grandeur of the place, now on a first name basis, he commented, "So this is where you live Carole, very impressive!"

"Yes Randy, it has everything. Won't you come in for a drink?"

Wisely declining, Summers beginning to realize Rosanoff was not what he pretended to be, "Thank you Carole, I'd better be getting back." After warmly Shaking hands, he left.

Meanwhile back in Montreal, Rosanoff was having a heated discussion with Gianni over Joey Palermo's intrusion into the Quebec drug market and what to do about it, forcibly telling Gianni he'd have New York take care of Palermo, upset on learning Summers had driven Carole back to the villa. Arriving back that evening, Rosanoff finding Carole sound asleep, not wanting to disturb her retired to the other bedroom.

He was awakened early the next morning by an upset Carole asking, "Why on earth did you sleep here?"

A still visibly disturbed Rosanoff replying sharply, "I didn't want to bother you. I thought you must have been tired after your return with that all Canadian boy Summers!"

"Oh David! You sound jealous! Well you have absolutely no reason to be. You're right dear compared to you he is a boy, you're a man, my man and I Love you. Now will you come to bed, our bed?"

He did, she making him very happy he had, they enjoying a very late breakfast.

CHAPTER 9

A Chance Meeting - The Enforcer and Maestro

Michael Reardon sitting at the Toronto Royal York Hotels cocktail lounge bar, idly swirling the ice cubes in a glass of scotch, awaiting a call from a downtown hotel owner confirming his decision to sell his hotel, having Reardon's real estate company, Orma Realty, find a buyer.

Just as Joey Palermo entered the lounge a page boy called out, "Mister Reardon, Mister Michael Reardon, a message for you."

Calling the boy over to the bar, tipped him taking from him a folded note, simply reading, 'Yes, go ahead. Confirming our arrangement in writing'. Smiling, turning back towards his drink. wincing when a strong hand gripped his right shoulder,

"Maestro! Mikey Reardon! Is it really you?"

Startled, Reardon turned around quickly in his stool, recognizing the voice's of the nattily dressed owner, "Joey, Joey Palermo, Enforcer! I don't believe it!"

"Come on Maestro let's find a quiet table." Settling at one in a corner, Palermo continued, "How long has it been Mikey, twenty or thirty years?"

"At least Joey, if not a few more, a lot of water under both our bridges since then."

"I don't understand Maestro why it's taken so long our being in the same city and all."

"Well Joey let's just say we traveled down different rivers, I suppose there wasn't any reason for us to."

"I guess you know Mikey, I stayed in the 'business' but now Big Time!"

"Yes Joey, I've read about you in the papers from time to time."

"Yeah, a few charges but no convictions!" Palermo proudly replied. "I read all about you in the papers too, wounded war hero, you even went to college. What are you doing now?"

"Real Estate, an army buddy of mine and I worked in my father's real estate business, Orma Realty, after we got out of the hospital, taking it over as partners when he died a few years ago."

"Orma Realty? I've heard of that business - big time in major property deals like hotels and businesses. I thought he was a druggist?"

"He was but started in Real Estate on the side until it became so profitable gave up being a pharmacist going into real estate full time."

Spending the next hour recalling the old days not saying very much about their current activities or private lives, staying that way until Palermo mentioning e was looking for a a small to medium sized downtown hotel for his 'business'.

Reardon enthusiastically replying, pulling the note given to him by the pager out of his jacket pocket,

"Joey I believe I Just have the one you're looking for, one that

I've just listed. It's called The Monte Carlo and is located on King Street, it has good gallonage, the rooms are decent and its small restaurant acceptable. More important the price could be right depending on the amount of upfront cash there is. The owner is in a real bind, he's just gone through a financially disastrous divorce over an affair with a money hungry cocktail waitress putting him badly in need of money."

"Sounds good Mikey I'll look it over with my lawyer. If he sees no problems we'll go ahead. It will be a cash deal with as little paperwork as possible, the less in my 'business' the better."

"Yes, I sort of gathered that, in mine it's essential. I'm heading back to my office to make sure my end of the deal with the owner is nailed down, for us Joey a handshake is enough."

"You mean no diversions this time Maestro?" he replied laughing.

"Good Lord, after all these years you haven't forgotten, Enforcer?"

"How could I Maestro? Using that is how I really got started in the 'business'!

Standing up they left, heading for the hotel's parking lot.

On arriving Reardon spotted a beautiful, new obviously very expensive Cadillac silver limousine, nudging Palermo commented, "Look at those great wheels Joey, there must be someone important inside."

"Not really Mikey, those wheels belong to me.!"

"To you? 'Business' must really be good!"

"Good Maestro? You have no idea. Look, why don't you give up this real estate nonsense and come into the 'business' with me? I could use a trustworthy partner like you? I'll even get you a car just like mine."

Smiling as they shook hands, Reardon replied, "Thanks all the same old friend, too much water has flowed under both our bridges, I wouldn't be of much use to you."

Sounding disappointed Palermo replied, "That's too bad. Look the offer is always open in case you change your mind."

The hotel deal was consummated a week later, all in cash, including Reardon's commission, substantially increased by a thankful Palermo, a factor mollifying the concerns of his partner Carr-Wilson, shocked at learning the identity of their client. At the conclusion of the transaction, Palermo and Reardon vigorously shaking hands, vowing to see each other again.

Two weeks later Joey Palermo was found stuffed awkwardly in the trunk of his beautiful silver Caddie in the airport parking lot with two bullet hole in his head, a professional Mafia hit!

CHAPTER 10

The Royal Canadian Mounted Police - Ronald Guthrie

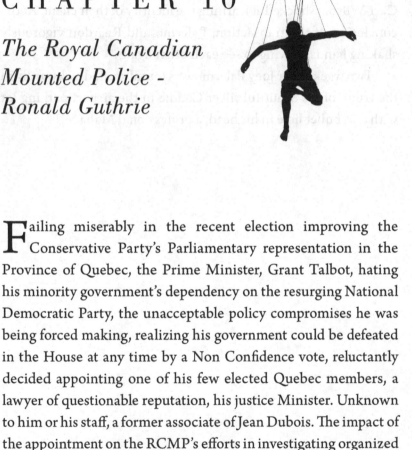

Failing miserably in the recent election improving the Conservative Party's Parliamentary representation in the Province of Quebec, the Prime Minister, Grant Talbot, hating his minority government's dependency on the resurging National Democratic Party, the unacceptable policy compromises he was being forced making, realizing his government could be defeated in the House at any time by a Non Confidence vote, reluctantly decided appointing one of his few elected Quebec members, a lawyer of questionable reputation, his justice Minister. Unknown to him or his staff, a former associate of Jean Dubois. The impact of the appointment on the RCMP's efforts in investigating organized crime in Canada wasn't long being felt, especially by the RCMP and its leading organized crime investigator, Inspector Ronald Guthrie, an incorruptible dedicated twenty year man.

Guthrie's ramrod bearing, red brush cut hair, bushy moustache, resembling a middle aged Prussian general at the turn of the of the 20th century. His piercing grey eyes, clipped speech, unnerved even the innocent when questioned by him. Believing Boris Aristine responsible for ordering the deaths of Nicky Gregorian and Scott Beaumont up to now unable to prove it, was skeptical at the report by French Security that Aristine had retired, questioned the identity of David Rosanoff despite strong documentation unquestionably supported its authenticity. He requested his superiors allowing him commencing a full scale investigation into Rosanoff, they in turn forwarding it to the Justice Department for approval.

Jean Dubois learning about this from a Justice department contact, met privately with the Justice Minister in his near Montreal riding, reminding the Minister of past favors including sizable financial support during past elections. Dubois demand the investigation be shut down occurred shortly after. Guthrie, quickly seconded to the External Affairs Department, assigned the thankless, time consuming task of leading a reorganization of the police force of a small West African nation.

This state of affairs existed until a series of missteps political and personal, forced the Prime Minster replacing his Justice Minister with a bright young lawyer MP from Alberta. Reviewing the departmental files, one of his aides happened upon the RCMP request for approval of the Rosanoff investigation. The Minister delving into the matter further on discovering Ronald Guthrie's excellent record, decided having him recalled to carrying out the investigation as well as recommending his promotion to Chief Inspector.

On his speedy return it didn't take Chief Inspector Guthrie to start working, immediately putting together a first class team of investigators. He intuitively wondered if the sudden Mafia style execution of Joey Palermo was an indication of a major problem in the Syndicate's upper echelon.

Jean Dubois made aware of Guthrie's reopening of the Aristine file by his Justice department contact was worried, not reporting this to Rosanoff but to Gianni, who in turn informed Silverberg in New York. Soon after, meeting in a secure location in New York, this time unaccompanied by Enforcers.

Gianni opening up the conversation, "Julius I'm really worried with Guthrie back into the act."

"Couldn't we just take him out Frankie?"

"Good Lord no Julius! You just don't take out a Mounted Police Chief Inspector. The heat on all of us would be unbearable"

"It's Aristine he's after. Right?"

"Yes Julius."

"The answer then is obvious, we take him out, we get rid of most of the heat."

A worried Gianni replying, "We'll have to take out Manoff along with him. I'm not sure I've got the right people to do it and what about our people in Paris, Naples and Sicily how are they going to take it?"

Silverberg replied, "The right people? Not your problem, I do, the best! As for the reaction of our people in Europe they're as concerned about Aristine's recent behavior as we are leaving its solution strictly in our hands. Aris- I mean Rosanoff is coming here shortly, unless something unexpected happens it will be a one way trip for him and his man."

"What about Toronto Julius, whose going to replace Palermo?"

"I have good reports on Palermo's cousin, Carlo Braganzi. He's been looking after business and doing a good job. It should please you Frankie, his father was Sicilian."

"Won't he want revenge for his cousin?"

"No, he's too smart for that. Besides he likes being the boss." Silverberg replied.

"What about Rosanoff's woman, could she be a problem?"

"I don't think so Frankie, she has no idea who he really is, should that happen you take care of it!" After discussing other business matters, Gianni left, returning to Montreal.

Meanwhile, Ronald Guthrie learned Rosanoff's true identity, not from the French Secret Police or Interpol, from the American Central Intelligence Agency concerned about the recent significant increase of drug shipments from Canada into the US, planned taking Rosanoff into custody for questioning at the first opportunity.

CHAPTER 11

Carole Learns the Truth

avid Rosanoff sensed something was wrong, his anxiety not relieved by Joey Palermo's exit in Toronto, noting Montreal's Gianni less communicative than usual, deciding to raise these issues at an upcoming meeting with the strongest arm of the Syndicate's North American operation, Julius Silverberg in New York. His anxiety further enhanced Carole receiving a Toronto phone call informing her of her mother suffering a complete nervous breakdown, begging to see her daughter. At first, Rosanoff refused a distraught Carole's pleading, until he received a call from her mother's doctor informing him of the seriousness of the situation, the crucial importance of Carole's presence in aiding her mother's recovery. He finally agreed, having Roger to drive her to Toronto, arranging for Carlo Braganzi keeping an eye on things, while she was there. These calls not unnoticed by Chief Inspector Ronald Guthrie, not only having the villa watched, managed tapping its phone line. He also arranged for a Toronto watch on the Masters' Rosedale residence.

Shortly after Carole's return to Toronto, Rosanoff relieved learning her return a real therapeutic help for her mother, reassured by Carole's nightly loving calls promised taking her on a month long cruise around the Mediterranean in a private yacht on her return to the villa. Not happy with Gianni lately virtually avoiding him, the troubles in Toronto not improved by Palermo's removal, sensing something wasn't right decided calling Dubois for a meeting to settle his affairs before leaving to meet with Silverberg. Shortly after Rosanoff left for New York accompanied by the ever present Cristoff both men never returning, Aristine really retired this time, with Manoff disappearing without a trace. Guthrie learning about this from his CIA contact, felt obliged informing Carole of this, at least for her, a tragic event. He decided to travel to Toronto doing this personally, thankful she was at her mother's home and not at the villa.

Arriving at the Masters' residence, ringing the door bell answered by Carole, who after he identified himself, seeing his grim look cried out, "Good Lord what's happened? Is it my David?"

"May I come in?"

"Of course, of course Chief Inspector, please excuse my rudeness, I could tell from your coming here and the look on you face something serious has happened." After seating themselves in the living room, she continued, catching her breath, "Has something happened to David? Is he dead?"

"Yes Miss Masters, I'm afraid so, I hate to have to tell you the truth about David Rosanoff at a time like this, it's better you hear it from me. His real name was Boris Aristine a notorious international drug dealer we believe responsible for ordering the killings of both Nick Gregorian and your husband."

"I don't believe it! It just can't be true!" she replied sobbing.

Waiting for her to settle down Guthrie continued, "I regret to say, I'm afraid it is."

Pausing, drying her eyes with a handkerchief he handed her, asking, "You knew about Nick and me?"

"Yes! We'd been watching him for some time knowing he was working for Aristine. It would be prudent for you staying here until things settle down. Although I don't believe you're in any danger I'm having a man keep a close watch on you just to be sure. If you have to leave the house for any reason one of my people will accompany you."

Carole offered to make coffee Guthrie politely declined saying he had to return to Ottawa but would keep in regular contact with her, leaving her a private number should she wish to call him at any time of the day or night.

CHAPTER 12

A New Beginning

A week later she received an urgent call from Jean Dubois, her phone number left with him by Aristine in case of an emergency. Having met him at one of his visits to the villa, told by her David Dubois was one of the few business associates he trusted. After receiving his condolences, responded cautiously, "Yes Mister Dubois, thank you, is there anything else?"

"There is about Mister Rosanoff's estate. I should meet with you in person as his lawyer discussing this, not over the phone. When would it be convenient for me to come to Toronto covering this very important matter with you?" Dubois asked.

"Yes of course Mister Dubois, this is a very difficult time for me, I'll let you know. Could you at least give me some idea of what you're talking about?"

"Yes, of course, I can tell you this. You are destined to become a very wealthy woman in addition left the Villa at Mont Tremblant and The Oasis in Ottawa." ending the conversation leaving her his number.

Carole immediately contacted Guthrie informing of this latest development he advising her to let a week go by before contacting Dubois enabling the RCMP getting a clearer idea of the impact of Aristine's death on the Montreal Syndicate. The impact quickly became evident with the sudden closing down of its drug front, the cosmetic import- export business both in Paris and Montreal, as well as shredding any documentation relating to Rosanoff, his money not in Canadian banks, being held in Switzerland numbered bank accounts. Counseled by Guthrie and her family lawyer Carole met with Dubois at her lawyer's office learning she was indeed a very wealthy woman, wealthy beyond her wildest dreams, soon learning such wealth entailed major responsibilities.

Meanwhile in Montreal, with the closing down of the cosmetic business, Randolph Summers was out of a job deciding to try his hand at teaching after a short search offered a position at a prestigious Toronto business school quickly accepting it moving to a comfortable apartment near the school, leaving a forwarding address with Dubois.

In her conversations with Guthrie at one point Carole asked him if Summers had any connection with the Syndicate's criminal activity. She was told absolutely not, that he had a very good business head, was a very capable manager. Badly needing the help of such a person Carole decided having her lawyer try to contact him which he did learning his Toronto address from Jean Dubois contacted him in the morning. A very surprised Randy Summers immensely pleased learning Carole Masters wanted to meet with him at her mother's home that afternoon.

Arriving at her door, Summers wearing a tweed jacket, brown corduroy slacks was met by a tired looking but still radiantly beautiful attractively dressed Carole Masters. Seated in the living room served coffee by a recently hired uniformed maid.

Avoiding any reference to Montreal, Rosanoff or the villa she quickly came to the point, "Randy I need the help of someone with a good business head on his shoulders, I've been told by several reliable sources you could be the one. It will entail a lot of responsibility but you'll be well paid."

A somewhat flustered embarrassed Summers replying, "That's very good of you Carole, I really can't. I've just accepted a teaching job, I just can't walk out on it."

"Of course not, so your first task will be t arrange for a sizeable contribution to be made to the school, that should more than make up for your leaving. What do you say Randy? The sooner we start the better with so much to be done. I'll arrange with my lawyer to draw up a contract."

Looking deeply into her eyes taking both her hands gently replied, "That won't be necessary, for us a handshake will be enough."

She breathlessly responding, "Yes! Yes! Remember our relationship will be strictly business!"

"Of course Carole, strictly business." both smiling, warmly shaking hands.

EPILOGUE

Ronald Guthrie was enjoying a drink with Tony Muldoon in the NDP member's House of Commons office having developed a close friendship with the former Ottawa Tribune's feature writer of the Dancing around the Hill political scene column, famous for his expose of the Gregorian Scandal, now an established presence in the National Democratic Party.

Muldoon refilling Guthrie's glass surmised, "Well Ron, the elimination of Aristine should put an end to the Syndicate business."

"I don't think so Tony." a skeptical Chief Inspector Guthrie replied toying with his drink.

"In heavens name why not, Ron?"

"Tony, the Syndicate is like a hydra snake, you cut off its head it quickly grows another one."

"Will you ever be able to end it then?"

"No Tony, not the police like me or the politicians like you can. It will only end when people stop buying the Syndicate's soul destroying products."

The End

Edward John Mastronardi